Wilder's Classic
One Acts

by Thornton Wilder

A SAMUEL FRENCH ACTING EDITION

FOUNDED 1830

SAMUELFRENCH.COM

MUSIC USE NOTE

Licensees are solely responsible for obtaining formal written permission from copyright owners to use copyrighted music in the performance of this play and are strongly cautioned to do so. If no such permission is obtained by the licensee, then the licensee must use only original music that the licensee owns and controls. Licensees are solely responsible and liable for all music clearances and shall indemnify the copyright owners of the play and their licensing agent, Samuel French, Inc., against any costs, expenses, losses and liabilities arising from the use of music by licensees.

IMPORTANT BILLING AND CREDIT
REQUIREMENTS

All producers of *WILDER'S CLASSIC ONE ACTS must* give credit to the Author of the Play in all programs distributed in connection with performances of the Play, and in all instances in which the title of the Play appears for the purposes of advertising, publicizing or otherwise exploiting the Play and/or a production. The name of the Author *must* appear on a separate line on which no other name appears, immediately following the title and *must* appear in size of type not less than fifty percent of the size of the title type.

INTRODUCTION TO
WILDER'S CLASSIC ONE ACTS

The six one act plays in this collection, celebrating different theatrical forms and moods, were first published by the thirty-four-year-old Thornton Wilder in 1931—in this country and in England—under the title, *The Long Christmas Dinner and Other Plays in One Act.* Today, with a bow to their place in twentieth-century drama, we call them *Wilder's Classic One Acts.*

Thornton Wilder always wanted to write plays—and wasted little time getting started. By the time he had graduated from college in 1920 he had already published some twenty pieces of short drama and one major play (to say nothing of being prodigiously well read in theater, haunting many a stage, and even serving a stint as a paid critic).

But when these six plays appeared, few beyond an inner-circle thought of him as a playwright. (*Our Town,* his first full-length drama to reach Broadway, still lay seven years in the future—opening February 4, 1938.) Everyone, however, knew Thornton Wilder as a novelist—the writer who had given the world three novels, among them the acclaimed 1927 Pulitzer Prize-winning *The Bridge of San Luis Rey.*

Wilder's lack of public status as a dramatist notwithstanding, fans of his fiction and others eagerly purchased his newest offering, and sales of *The Long Christmas Dinner and Other Plays in One Act* were strong. (It could not have hurt sales that the influential *New York Times* reviewer Percy Hutchison found several plays in the volume "very near to miniature masterpieces.") Plays, of course, show best when performed, and after Samuel French added Wilder's titles to its list in 1932, productions of *The Long Christmas Dinner, The Happy Journey to Trenton and Camden, Pullman Car Hiawatha, Love and How to Cure It, Queens of France,* and *Such Things Only Happen in Books* began springing up across the country and in England.

Although written for schools and community playhouses, the official record of these plays—with the exception of *Such Things Only Happen in Books**—includes stock and professional productions, adaptations for radio, television, and in the case of *The Long Christmas Dinner,* even opera. Perhaps the most high-profile production of any of the six was the successful Broadway run of *The Happy Journey to Trenton and Camden,* performed as a

---

* When it was first produced, Wilder described *Such Things Only Happen in Books,* a play he purposely (and playfully) constructed in a conventional form, as "an attempt to see how many plots may be worked into one act." By the late 1930s, for reasons never explained, he had withdrawn it. It remained in this status until 1997 when Wilder's literary executor restored it to the Wilder canon.

curtain-raiser for Jean-Paul Sartre's *The Respectful Prostitute* in 1947. We should not be surprised, given their stature, that over the past half-century several of Wilder's six one acts have turned up regularly Off Broadway, winning critical acclaim and awards.

Students of American drama have long recognized that the three most "cosmic" ("modernist") of these works—*The Long Christmas Dinner*, *The Happy Journey to Trenton and Camden*, and *Pullman Car Hiawatha*—as well as the farcical *Queens of France*, contain examples of the techniques and devices that Wilder would later employ in his four major plays: *Our Town*, *The Matchmaker*, *The Skin of our Teeth*, and *The Alcestiad*. In these one acts we find Wilder experimenting with such innovative ideas as the stage-manager as a visible and engaged character, non-linear time schemes, the banishment of literal scenery, and elements drawn from farce and Classical theater. When performing Wilder's one acts, actors find themselves handling the theatrical tools with which a lasting chapter in the history of twentieth-century drama was written.

But the reason for producing these plays is not their role in Thornton Wilder's artistic future, as arresting as that role may be. The enormous success of *Wilder's Classic One Acts* over the years speaks to the more important reason: that these short pieces of drama play wonderfully well in their own right as polished and masterful representatives of drama in the compressed form.

***

Samuel French and the Wilder family take great pleasure and pride in celebrating *Wilder's Classics One Acts*, now in their eighth decade, by reissuing them in new collected and individual acting editions. For additional information about these plays, we invite you to visit www.thorntonwilder.com.

Tappan Wilder
Literary Executor for Thornton Wilder

CONTENTS

THE LONG CHRISTMAS DINNER

CHARACTERS

LUCIA, Roderick's wife
RODERICK, Mother Bayard's son
MOTHER BAYARD
COUSIN BRANDON
CHARLES, Lucia and Roderick's son
GENEVIEVE, Lucia and Roderick's daughter
LEONORA BANNING, Charles's wife
LUCIA, Leonora and Charles's daughter, Samuel's twin
SAMUEL, Leonora and Charles's son, Lucia's twin
RODERICK, Leonora and Charles's youngest son
COUSIN ERMENGARDE
SERVANTS
NURSES

THE SCENE

The dining room of the Bayard home. A long dining table is handsomely spread for Christmas dinner. The carver's place with a great turkey before it is at the right. Down left, by the proscenium arch, is a strange portal trimmed with garlands of fruits and flowers. Directly opposite, down right, is another portal hung with black velvet. The portals denote birth and death, respectively.

Along the rear wall, at the right, is a sideboard, in the center a fireplace with perhaps a portrait of a man above it, and on the left a large door into the hall.

At the table there is a chair at each end, and three chairs against the walls. The chair at the head of the table should be high-backed and with arms.

NOTES FOR THE PRODUCER

Ninety years are traversed in this play which represents in accelerated motion ninety Christmas dinners in the Bayard household. Although the speech, the manner and business of the actors is colloquial and realistic, the production should stimulate the imagination and be implied and suggestive. Accordingly gray curtains with set pieces are recommended for the walls of the room rather than conventional scenery. In the center of the table is a bowl of Christmas greens and at the left end a wine decanter and glasses. Except for these all properties in the play are imaginary. Throughout the play the characters continue eating invisible food with imaginary knives and forks. The actors are dressed in inconspicuous clothes and must indicate their gradual increase in years through their acting.

The ladies may have shawls concealed which they gradually draw up about their shoulders as they grow older.

At the rise of the curtain the stage should be dark, gradually a bright light dims on and covers the table. Floods of light also are directed on the stage from the two portals. The flood from stage Right should be a "cool" color, and the one from stage Left "warm." If possible all lights should be kept off the walls of the room. (It may be possible, when this play is given by itself, to dispense with the curtain, so that the audience arriving will see the stage set and the table laid, though in indistinct darkness.)

Experience has shown that many companies have fallen into the practice of playing this play in a weird, lugubrious manner. Care should be taken that the conversation is normal and that after the "deaths" the play should pick up its tempo at once.

(There is no curtain. The audience arriving at the theatre sees the stage set and the table laid, though still in partial darkness. Gradually the lights in the auditorium become dim and the stage brightens until sparkling winter sunlight streams through the dining-room windows. Enter **LUCIA** *from the hall. She inspects the table, touching here a knife and there a fork. She talks to a servant girl who is invisible to us.)*

LUCIA. I reckon we're ready now, Gertrude. We won't ring the chimes today. I'll just call them myself. *(She goes into the hall and calls.)* Roderick. Mother Bayard. We're all ready. Come to dinner.

(Enter **RODERICK** *pushing* **MOTHER BAYARD** *in a wheelchair.)*

MOTHER BAYARD. ...and a new horse too, Roderick. I used to think that only the wicked owned two horses. A new horse and a new house and a new wife!

LUCIA. Here, Mother Bayard, you sit between us.

RODERICK. Well, Mother, how do you like it? Our first Christmas dinner in the new house, hey?

MOTHER BAYARD. Tz-Tz-Tz! I don't know what your dear father would say!

*(***RODERICK*** says grace.)*

My dear Lucia, I can remember when there were still Indians on this very ground, and I wasn't a young girl either. I can remember when we had to cross the Mississippi on a new-made raft. I can remember when Saint Louis and Kansas City were full of Indians.

LUCIA. *(tying a napkin around* **MOTHER BAYARD**'s *neck)* Imagine that! There! What a wonderful day for our first Christmas dinner: a beautiful sunny morning, snow, a splendid sermon. Dr. McCarthy preaches a splendid sermon. I cried and cried.

13

RODERICK. *(extending an imaginary carving fork)* Come now, what'll you have, Mother? A little sliver of white?

LUCIA. Every last twig is wrapped around with ice. You almost never see that. Can I cut it up for you, dear? *(over her shoulder)* Gertrude, I forgot the jelly. You know – on the top shelf. Mother Bayard, I found your mother's gravy boat while we were moving. What was her name, dear? What were all your names? You were…a… Genevieve Wainright. Now your mother –

MOTHER BAYARD. Yes, you must write it down somewhere. I was Genevieve Wainright. My mother was Faith Morrison. She was the daughter of a farmer in New Hampshire who was something of a blacksmith too. And she married young John Wainright –

LUCIA. *(memorizing on her fingers)* Genevieve Wainright. Faith Morrison.

RODERICK. It's all down in a book somewhere upstairs. We have it all. All that kind of thing is very interesting. Come, Lucia, just a little wine. Mother, a little red wine for Christmas day. Full of iron. "Take a little wine for thy stomach's sake."

LUCIA. Really, I can't get used to wine! What would my father say? But I suppose it's all right.

(Enter COUSIN BRANDON *from the hall. He takes his place by* LUCIA.*)*

COUSIN BRANDON. *(rubbing his hands)* Well, well, I smell turkey. My dear cousins, I can't tell you how pleasant it is to be having Christmas dinner with you all. I've lived out there in Alaska so long without relatives. Let me see, how long have you had this new house, Roderick?

RODERICK. Why, it must be…

MOTHER BAYARD. Five years. It's five years, children. You should keep a diary. This is your sixth Christmas dinner here.

LUCIA. Think of that, Roderick. We feel as though we had lived here twenty years.

COUSIN BRANDON. At all events it still looks as good as new.

RODERICK. *(over his carving)* What'll you have, Brandon, light or dark? – Frieda, fill up Cousin Brandon's glass.

LUCIA. Oh, dear, I can't get used to these wines. I don't know what my father'd say, I'm sure. What'll you have, Mother Bayard?

(During the following speeches **MOTHER BAYARD** *'s chair, without any visible propulsion, starts to draw away from the table, turns toward the right, and slowly goes toward the right portal.)*

MOTHER BAYARD. Yes, I can remember when there were Indians on this very land.

LUCIA. *(softly)* Mother Bayard hasn't been very well lately, Roderick.

MOTHER BAYARD. My mother was a Faith Morrison. And in New Hampshire she married a young John Wainright, who was a congregational minister. He saw her in his congregation one day...

LUCIA. *(rising and coming to center stage)* Mother Bayard, hadn't you better lie down, dear?

MOTHER BAYARD. ...and right in the middle of his sermon he said to himself: "I'll marry that girl." And he did, and I'm their daughter.

*(***RODERICK*** *rises, turns to right with concern.)*

LUCIA. *(looking after her with anxiety)* Just a little nap, dear?

MOTHER BAYARD. I'm all right. Just go on with your dinner. *(exit right)* I was ten, and I said to my brother...

(A very slight pause during which **RODERICK** *sits and* **LUCIA** *returns to her seat. All three resume eating.)*

COUSIN BRANDON. *(genially)* It's too bad it's such a cold dark day today. We almost need the lamps. I spoke to Major Lewis for a moment after church. His sciatica troubles him, but he does pretty well.

LUCIA. *(dabbing her eyes)* I know Mother Bayard wouldn't want us to grieve for her on Christmas Day, but I can't forget her sitting in her wheelchair right beside us, only a year ago. And she would be so glad to know our good news.

RODERICK. Now, now. It's Christmas. (*formally*) Cousin Brandon, a glass of wine with you, sir.

COUSIN BRANDON. (*half rising, lifting his glass gallantly*) A glass of wine with you, sir.

LUCIA. Does the Major's sciatica cause him much pain?

COUSIN BRANDON. Some, perhaps. But you know his way. He says it'll be all the same in a hundred years.

LUCIA. Yes, he's a great philosopher.

RODERICK. His wife sends you a thousand thanks for her Christmas present.

LUCIA. I forget what I gave her. – Oh, yes, the workbasket!

(*Slight pause. Characters look toward the left portal. Through the entrance of Birth comes a* **NURSE** *holding in her arms an imaginary baby.* **LUCIA** *rushes toward it, the men following.*)

O my wonderful new baby, my darling baby! Who ever saw such a child! Quick, nurse, a boy or a girl? A boy! Roderick, what shall we call him? Really, nurse, you've never seen such a child!

RODERICK. We'll call him Charles after your father and grandfather.

LUCIA. But there are no Charleses in the Bible, Roderick.

RODERICK. Of course, there are. Surely there are.

LUCIA. Roderick! – Very well, but he will always be Samuel to me.

COUSIN BRANDON. Really, Nurse, you've never seen such a child.

(**NURSE** *starts up stage to center door.*)

LUCIA. What miraculous hands he has! Really, they are the most beautiful hands in the world. All right, nurse. Have a good nap, my darling child.

(*Exit* **NURSE** *in the hall.* **LUCIA** *and* **COUSIN BRANDON** *to seats.*)

RODERICK. (*calling through center door*) Don't drop him, nurse. Brandon and I need him in our firm.
Lucia, a little white meat? Some stuffing? Cranberry sauce, anybody?

LUCIA. *(over her shoulder)* Margaret, the stuffing is very good today. – Just a little, thank you.

RODERICK. Now something to wash it down. *(half rising)* Cousin Brandon, a glass of wine with you, sir. To the ladies, God bless them.

LUCIA. Thank you, kind sirs.

COUSIN BRANDON. Pity it's such an overcast day today. And no snow.

LUCIA. But the sermon was lovely. I cried and cried. Dr. Spaulding does preach such a splendid sermon.

RODERICK. I saw Major Lewis for a moment after church. He says his rheumatism comes and goes. His wife says she has something for Charles and will bring it over this afternoon.

(Again they turn to the portal down left. Enter **NURSE** *as before.* **LUCIA** *rushes to her.* **RODERICK** *comes to center of stage below table.* **COUSIN BRANDON** *does not rise.)*

LUCIA. O my lovely new baby! Really, it never occurred to me that it might be a girl. Why, nurse, she's perfect.

RODERICK. Now call her what you choose. It's your turn.

LUCIA. Loolooloo. Aië. Aië. Yes, this time I shall have my way. She shall be called Genevieve after your mother. Have a good nap, my treasure.

(Exit **NURSE** *into the hall.)*

Imagine! Sometime she'll be grown up and say "Good morning, Mother. Good morning, Father." – Really, Cousin Brandon, you don't find a baby like that every day.

(They return to their seats and again begin to eat. **RODERICK** *carves as before, standing.)*

COUSIN BRANDON. *And* the new factory.

LUCIA. A new factory? Really? Roderick, I shall be very uncomfortable if we're going to turn out to be rich. I've been afraid of that for years. – However, we mustn't talk about such things on Christmas Day. I'll just take a little piece of white meat, thank you. Roderick, Charles is destined for the ministry. I'm sure of it.

RODERICK. Woman, he's only twelve. Let him have a free mind. *We* want him in the firm, I don't mind saying.

(He sits. Definitely shows maturity.)

Anyway, no time passes as slowly as this when you're waiting for your urchins to grow up and settle down to business.

LUCIA. I don't want time to go any faster, thank you. I love the children just as they are. – Really, Roderick, you know what the doctor said: one glass a meal. No, Margaret, that will be all.

*(**RODERICK** rises, glass in hand. With a look of dismay on his face he takes a few steps toward the right portal.)*

RODERICK. *(glass in hand)* Now I wonder what's the matter with me.

LUCIA. Roderick, do be reasonable.

RODERICK. *(rises, takes a few steps right with gallant irony)* But, my dear, statistics show that we steady, moderate drinkers…

LUCIA. *(rises, rushes to center below table)* Roderick! My dear! What…?

RODERICK. *(returns to his seat with a frightened look of relief; now definitely older)* Well, it's fine to be back at table with you again.

*(**LUCIA** returns to her seat.)*

How many good Christmas dinners have I had to miss upstairs? And to be back at a fine bright one, too.

LUCIA. O my dear, you gave us a very alarming time! Here's your glass of milk. – Josephine, bring Mr. Bayard his medicine from the cupboard in the library.

RODERICK. At all events, now that I'm better I'm going to start doing something about the house.

LUCIA. Roderick! You're not going to change the house?

RODERICK. Only touch it up here and there. It looks a hundred years old.

(CHARLES enters casually from the hall.)

CHARLES. It's a great blowy morning, Mother. The wind comes over the hill like a lot of cannon. *(He kisses his mother's hair.)*

LUCIA. Charles, you carve the turkey, dear. Your father's not well.

RODERICK. But - not yet.

CHARLES. You always said you hated carving.

(CHARLES gets a chair from right wall and puts it right end of table where MOTHER BAYARD was. RODERICK sits. CHARLES takes his father's former place at the end of the table. CHARLES, sitting, begins to carve.)

LUCIA. *(showing her years)* And such a good sermon. I cried and cried. Mother Bayard loved a good sermon so. And she used to sing the Christmas hymns all around the year. Oh, dear, oh, dear, I've been thinking of her all morning!

CHARLES. Shh, Mother. It's Christmas Day. You mustn't think of such things. You mustn't be depressed.

LUCIA. But sad things aren't the same as depressing things. I must be getting old: I like them.

CHARLES. Uncle Brandon, you haven't anything to eat. Pass his plate, Hilda...and some cranberry sauce...

(Enter GENEVIEVE from the hall.)

GENEVIEVE. It's glorious. *(kisses father's temple, gets chair and sits center between her father and COUSIN BRANDON)* Every last twig is wrapped around with ice. You almost never see that.

LUCIA. Did you have time to deliver those presents after church, Genevieve?

GENEVIEVE. Yes, Mama. Old Mrs. Lewis sends you a thousand thanks for hers. It was just what she wanted, she said. Give me lots, Charles, lots.

RODERICK. Statistics, ladies and gentlemen, show that we steady, moderate...

CHARLES. How about a little skating this afternoon, Father?

RODERICK. I'll live till I'm ninety. *(rising and starting toward right portal)*

LUCIA. I really don't think he ought to go skating.

RODERICK. *(at the very portal, suddenly astonished)* Yes, but... but...not yet!

(He goes out.)

LUCIA. *(dabbing her eyes)* He was so young and so clever, Cousin Brandon. *(raising her voice for* **COUSIN BRANDON***'s deafness)* I say he was so young and so clever. – Never forget your father, children. He was a good man. Well, he wouldn't want us to grieve for him today.

CHARLES. White or dark, Genevieve? Just another sliver, Mother?

LUCIA. *(drawing on her shawl)* I can remember our first Christmas dinner in this house, Genevieve. Twenty-five years ago today. Mother Bayard was sitting here in her wheelchair. She could remember when Indians lived on this very spot and when she had to cross the river on a new-made raft.

CHARLES. She couldn't have, Mother.

GENEVIEVE. That can't be true.

LUCIA. It certainly was true – even I can remember when there was only one paved street. We were very happy to walk on boards. *(louder, to* **COUSIN BRANDON***)* We can remember when there were no sidewalks, can't we, Cousin Brandon?

COUSIN BRANDON. *(delighted)* Oh, yes! And those were the days.

CHARLES & GENEVIEVE. *(sotto voce, this is a family refrain)* Those were the days.

LUCIA. ...and the ball last night, Genevieve? Did you have a nice time? I hope you didn't *waltz*, dear. I think a girl in our position ought to set an example. Did Charles keep an eye on you?

GENEVIEVE. He had none left. They were all on Leonora Banning. He can't conceal it any longer, Mother. I think he's engaged to marry Leonora Banning.

CHARLES. I'm not engaged to marry anyone.

LUCIA. Well, she's very pretty.

GENEVIEVE. I shall never marry, Mother. – I shall sit in this house beside you forever, as though life were one long, happy Christmas dinner.

LUCIA. O my child, you mustn't say such things!

GENEVIEVE. *(playfully)* You don't want me? You don't want me?

(LUCIA bursts into tears. GENEVIEVE rises and goes to her.)

Why, Mother, how silly you are! There's nothing sad about that – what could possibly be sad about that?

LUCIA. *(drying her eyes)* Forgive me. I'm just unpredictable, that's all.

(CHARLES goes to the door and leads in LEONORA BANNING from the hall.)

CHARLES. Leonora!

LEONORA. Good morning, Mother Bayard.

(LUCIA rises and greets LEONORA near the door. COUSIN BRANDON also rises.)

Good morning, everybody. Mother Bayard, you sit here by Charles.

(She helps her into chair formerly occupied by RODERICK. COUSIN BRANDON sits in center chair. GENEVIEVE sits on his left, and LEONORA sits at foot of the table.)

It's really a splendid Christmas Day today.

CHARLES. Little white meat? Genevieve, Mother, Leonora?

LEONORA. Every last twig is encircled with ice. – You never see that.

CHARLES. *(shouting)* Uncle Brandon, another? – Rogers, fill my uncle's glass.

LUCIA. *(to* **CHARLES***)* Do what your father used to do. It would please Cousin Brandon so. You know *(pretending to raise a glass)* "Uncle Brandon, a glass of wine…"

CHARLES. *(rising)* Uncle Brandon, a glass of wine with you, sir.

COUSIN BRANDON. A glass of wine with you, sir. To the ladies, God bless them every one.

THE LADIES. Thank you, kind sirs.

GENEVIEVE. And if I go to Germany for my music I promise to be back for Christmas. I wouldn't miss that.

LUCIA. I hate to think of you over there all alone in those strange pensions.

GENEVIEVE. But, darling, the time will pass so fast that you'll hardly know I'm gone. I'll be back in the twinkling of an eye.

*(***LEONORA*** looks toward left portal, rises, takes several steps. ***NURSE*** enters, with baby, down left.)*

LEONORA. Oh, what an angel! The darlingest baby in the world. Do let me hold it, nurse.

*(The ***NURSE*** resolutely has been crossing the stage and now exits at the right portal. ***LEONORA*** follows.)*

Oh, I did love it so!

*(***CHARLES*** rises, puts his arm around his wife, whispering, and slowly leads her back to her chair.)*

GENEVIEVE. *(softly to her mother as the other two cross)* Isn't there anything I can do?

LUCIA. *(raises her eyebrows, ruefully)* No, dear. Only time, only the passing of time can help in these things.

*(***CHARLES*** returns to his seat. Slight pause.)*

Don't you think we could ask Cousin Ermengarde to come and live with us here? There's plenty for everyone and there's no reason why she should go on teaching the first grade for ever and ever. She wouldn't be in the way, would she, Charles?

CHARLES. No, I think it would be fine. – A little more potato and gravy, anybody? A little more turkey, Mother?

(COUSIN BRANDON rises and starts slowly toward the right portal. LUCIA rises and stands for a moment with her face in her hands.)

COUSIN BRANDON. *(muttering)* It was great to be in Alaska in those days…

GENEVIEVE. *(half rising, and gazing at her mother in fear)* Mother, what is…?

LUCIA. *(hurriedly)* Hush, my dear. It will pass. – Hold fast to your music, you know. *(as GENEVIEVE starts toward her)* No, no. I want to be alone for a few minutes.

CHARLES. If the Republicans collected all their votes instead of going off into cliques among themselves, they might prevent his getting a second term.

(LUCIA turns and starts after COUSIN BRANDON toward the right.)

GENEVIEVE. Charles, Mother doesn't tell us, but she hasn't been very well these days.

CHARLES. Come, Mother, we'll go to Florida for a few weeks.

(GENEVIEVE rushes toward her mother.)

(Exit COUSIN BRANDON right.)

LUCIA. *(by the portal, smiling at GENEVIEVE and waving her hand)* Don't be foolish. Don't grieve.

(LUCIA clasps her hands under her chin. Her lips move, whispering. She walks serenely into the portal.)

GENEVIEVE. *(stares after her)* But what will I do? What's left for me to do?

(She returns to her seat.)

(At the same moment the NURSE, with two babies, enters from the left. LEONORA rushes to them.)

LEONORA. O my darlings…twins…Charles, aren't they glorious! Look at them. Look at them. **(CHARLES** *crosses down left.)*

CHARLES. *(bending over the basket)* Which is which?

LEONORA. I feel as though I were the first mother who ever had twins. – Look at them now! But why wasn't Mother Bayard allowed to stay and see them!

GENEVIEVE. *(rising suddenly distraught, loudly)* I don't want to go on. I can't bear it.

CHARLES. *(Goes to her quickly. They sit down. He whispers to her earnestly, taking both her hands.)* But Genevieve, Genevieve! How frightfully Mother would feel to think that…Genevieve!

GENEVIEVE. *(wildly)* I never told her how wonderful she was. We all treated her as though she were just a friend in the house. I thought she'd be here forever. *(sits)*

LEONORA. *(timidly)* Genevieve darling, do come one minute and hold my babies' hands.

(**GENEVIEVE** *collects herself and goes over to the* **NURSE.** *She smiles brokenly into the basket.)*

We shall call the girl Lucia after her grandmother – will that please you? Do just see what adorable little hands they have.

GENEVIEVE. They are wonderful, Leonora.

LEONORA. Give him your finger, darling. Just let him hold it.

CHARLES. And we'll call the boy Samuel. – Well, now everybody come and finish your dinners.

(The women take their places. The **NURSE** *exits into the hall.* **CHARLES** *calls out.)*

Don't drop them, nurse; at least don't drop the boy. We need him in the firm.

(He returns to his place.)

LEONORA. Someday they'll be big. Imagine! They'll come in and say "Hello, Mother!"

CHARLES. *(now forty, dignified)* Come, a little wine, Leonora, Genevieve? Full of iron. Eduardo, fill the ladies' glasses. It certainly is a keen, cold morning. I used to go skating with Father on mornings like this and Mother would come back from church saying –

GENEVIEVE. *(dreamily)* I know: saying, "Such a splendid sermon. I cried and cried."

LEONORA. Why did she cry, dear?

GENEVIEVE. That generation all cried at sermons. It was their way.

LEONORA. Really, Genevieve?

GENEVIEVE. They had had to go since they were children and I suppose sermons reminded them of their fathers and mothers, just as Christmas dinners do us. Especially in an old house like this.

LEONORA. It really is pretty old, Charles. And so ugly, with all that ironwork filigree and that dreadful cupola.

GENEVIEVE. Charles! You aren't going to change the house!

CHARLES. No, no. I won't give up the house, but great heavens! It's fifty years old. This spring we'll remove the cupola and build a new wing toward the tennis courts.

*(From now on **GENEVIEVE** is seen to change. She sits up more straightly. The corners of her mouth become fixed. She becomes a forthright and slightly disillusioned spinster. **CHARLES** becomes the plain businessman and a little pompous.)*

LEONORA. And then couldn't we ask your dear old Cousin Ermengarde to come and live with us? She's really the self-effacing kind.

CHARLES. Ask her now. Take her out of the first grade.

GENEVIEVE. We only seem to think of it on Christmas Day with her Christmas card staring us in the face.

*(Enter left, **NURSE** and baby.)*

LEONORA. Another boy! Another boy! Here's a Roderick for you at last.

CHARLES. *(crossing down left)* Roderick Brandon Bayard. A regular little fighter.

LEONORA. Goodbye, darling. Don't grow up too fast. Yes, yes. Aie, aie, aie – stay just as you are. Thank you, nurse.

GENEVIEVE. *(who has not left the table, repeats dryly)* Stay just as you are.

*(Exit **NURSE** into the hall. **CHARLES** and **LEONORA** return to their places.)*

LEONORA. Now I have three children. One, two, three. Two boys and a girl. I'm collecting them. It's very exciting. *(over her shoulder)* What, Hilda? Oh, Cousin Ermengarde's come! Come in, Cousin.

*(She goes to the hall door and welcomes **COUSIN ERMENGARDE**, already an elderly woman.)*

ERMENGARDE. *(shyly)* It's such a pleasure to be with you all.

CHARLES. *(pulling out the center chair for her)* The twins have taken a great fancy to you already, Cousin.

LEONORA. The baby went to her at once.

CHARLES. Exactly how are we related, Cousin Ermengarde? – There, Genevieve, that's your specialty. – First a little more turkey and stuffing, Mother? Cranberry sauce, anybody?

GENEVIEVE. I can work it out: Grandmother Bayard was your...

ERMENGARDE. Your Grandmother Bayard was a second cousin of my Grandmother Haskins through the Wainrights.

CHARLES. Well, it's all in a book somewhere upstairs. All that kind of thing is awfully interesting.

GENEVIEVE. Nonsense. There are no such books. I collect my notes off gravestones, and you have to scrape a good deal of moss – let me tell you – to find one great-grandparent.

CHARLES. There's a story that my Grandmother Bayard crossed the Mississippi on a raft before there were any bridges or ferryboats. She died before Genevieve and I were born. Time certainly goes very fast in a great new country like this. Have some more cranberry sauce, Cousin Ermengarde.

ERMENGARDE. *(timidly)* Well, time must be passing very slowly in Europe with this dreadful, dreadful war going on.

CHARLES. Perhaps an occasional war isn't so bad after all. It clears up a lot of poisons that collect in nations. It's like a boil.

ERMENGARDE. Oh, dear, oh, dear!

CHARLES. *(with relish)* Yes, it's like a boil. – Ho! Ho! Here are your twins.

(The twins appear at the door into the hall. SAM is wearing the uniform of an ensign. LUCIA is fussing over some detail on it.)

LUCIA. Isn't he wonderful in it, Mother?

CHARLES. Let's get a look at you.

SAM. Mother, don't let Roderick fool with my stamp album while I'm gone. *(crosses to the right)*

LEONORA. Now, Sam, do write a letter once in a while. Do be a good boy about that, mind.

SAM. You might send some of those cakes of yours once in a while, Cousin Ermengarde.

(LEONORA rises)

ERMENGARDE. *(in a flutter)* I certainly will, my dear boy.

(LEONORA crosses to center. SAM crosses down right.)

CHARLES. *(rising and facing SAM.)* If you need any money, we have agents in Paris and London, remember.

LEONORA. *(crossing down right)* Do be a good boy, Sam.

SAM. Well, good-bye…

(SAM kisses his mother without sentimentality and goes out briskly through the right portal. They all return to their seats, LUCIA sitting at her father's left.)

ERMENGARDE. *(in a low, constrained voice, making conversation)* I spoke to Mrs. Fairchild for a moment coming out of church. Her rheumatism's a little better, she says. She sends you her warmest thanks for the Christmas present. The workbasket, wasn't it? *(slight pause)* – It was an admirable sermon. And our stained-glass window looked so beautiful, Leonora, so beautiful. Everybody spoke of it and so affectionately of Sammy.

*(**LEONORA**'s hand goes to her mouth.)*

Forgive me, Leonora, but it's better to speak of him than not to speak of him when we're all thinking of him so hard.

LEONORA. *(rising, in anguish)* He was a mere boy. He was a mere boy, Charles.

CHARLES. My dear, my dear.

LEONORA. I want to tell him how wonderful he was. We let him go so casually. I want to tell him how we all feel about him. – Forgive me, let me walk about a minute. – Yes, of course, Ermengarde – it's best to speak of him.

LUCIA. *(in a low voice to **GENEVIEVE**)* Isn't there anything I can do?

GENEVIEVE. No, no. Only time, only the passing of time can help in these things.

*(**LEONORA**, straying about the room, finds herself near the door to the hall at the moment that her son **RODERICK** enters. He links his arm with hers and leads her back to the table. He looks up and sees the family's dejection.)*

RODERICK. What's the matter, anyway? What are you so glum about? The skating was fine today.

CHARLES. Roderick, I have something to say to you.

RODERICK. *(standing below his mother's chair)* Everybody was there. Lucia skated in the corners with Dan Creighton the whole time. When'll it be, Lucia, when'll it be?

LUCIA. I don't know what you mean.

RODERICK. Lucia's leaving us soon, Mother. Dan Creighton, of all people.

CHARLES. *(ominously)* Young man, I have something to say to you.

RODERICK. Yes, Father.

CHARLES. Is it true, Roderick, that you made yourself conspicuous last night at the Country Club – at a Christmas Eve dance, too?

LEONORA. Not now, Charles, I beg of you. This is Christmas dinner.

RODERICK. *(loudly)* No, I didn't.

LUCIA. Really, Father, he didn't. It was that dreadful Johnny Lewis.

CHARLES. I don't want to hear about Johnny Lewis. I want to know whether a son of mine...

LEONORA. Charles, I beg of you...

CHARLES. The first family of this city!

RODERICK. *(crossing below table to left center)* I hate this town and everything about it. I always did.

CHARLES. You behaved like a spoiled puppy, sir, an ill-bred spoiled puppy.

RODERICK. What did I do? What did I do that was wrong?

CHARLES. *(rising)* You were drunk and you were rude to the daughters of my best friends.

GENEVIEVE. *(striking the table)* Nothing in the world deserves an ugly scene like this. Charles, I'm ashamed of you.

RODERICK. Great God, you gotta get drunk in this town to forget how dull it is. Time passes so slowly here that it stands still, that's what's the trouble. *(turns and walks toward the hall door)*

CHARLES. Well, young man, we can employ your time. You will leave the university and you will come into the Bayard factory on January second.

RODERICK. *(at the door into the hall)* I have better things to do than to go into your old factory. I'm going somewhere where time passes, my God!

(He goes out into the hall.)

LEONORA. *(rising and rushing to the door)* Roderick, Roderick, come here just a moment. – Charles where can he go?

LUCIA. *(rising)* Shh, Mother. He'll come back.

(She leads her mother back to chair then starts for the hall door.)

Now I have to go upstairs and pack my trunk.

LEONORA. I won't have any children left! *(sits)*

LUCIA. *(from the door)* Shh, Mother. He'll come back. He's only gone to California or somewhere. Cousin Ermengarde has done most of my packing – thanks a thousand times, Cousin Ermengarde. *(She kisses her mother as an afterthought.)* I won't be long.

(She runs out into the hall.)

ERMENGARDE. *(cheerfully)* It's a very beautiful day. On the way home from church I stopped and saw Mrs. Foster a moment. Her arthritis comes and goes.

LEONORA. Is she actually in pain, dear?

ERMENGARDE. Oh, she says it'll all be the same in a hundred years!

LEONORA. Yes, she's a brave little stoic.

CHARLES. Come now, a little white meat, Mother? – Mary, pass my cousin's plate.

LEONORA. What is it, Mary? – Oh, here's a telegram from them in Paris! "Love and Christmas greetings to all." I told them we'd be eating some of their wedding cake and thinking about them today. It seems to be all decided that they will settle down in the east, Ermengarde. I can't even have my daughter for a neighbor. They hope to build before long somewhere on the shore north of New York.

GENEVIEVE. There is no shore north of New York.

LEONORA. Well, east or west or whatever it is.

(pause)

CHARLES. *(now sixty years old)* My, what a dark day. How slowly time passes without any young people in the house.

LEONORA. I have three children somewhere.

CHARLES. *(blunderingly offering comfort)* Well, one of them gave his life for his country.

LEONORA. *(sadly)* And one of them is selling aluminum in China.

GENEVIEVE. *(slowly working herself up to a hysterical crisis)* I can stand everything but this terrible soot everywhere. We should have moved long ago. We're surrounded by factories. We have to change the window curtains every week.

LEONORA. Why, Genevieve!

GENEVIEVE. I can't stand it. *(rising)* I can't stand it any more. I'm going abroad. It's not only the soot that comes through the very walls of this house; it's the *thoughts*, it's the thought of what has been and what might have been here. And the feeling about this house of the years *grinding away*. My mother died yesterday – not twenty-five years ago. Oh, I'm going to live and die abroad!

*(***CHARLES*** rises.)*

Yes, I'm going to be the American old maid living and dying in a pension in Munich or Florence.

ERMENGARDE. Genevieve, you're tired.

CHARLES. Come, Genevieve, take a good drink of cold water. Mary, open the window a minute.

GENEVIEVE. I'm sorry. I'm sorry.

*(***GENEVIEVE*** *hurries tearfully out into the hall.* ***CHARLES*** *sits.)*

ERMENGARDE. Dear Genevieve will come back to us, I think.

(She rises and starts toward the right portal.)

You should have been out today, Leonora. It was one of those days when everything was encircled with ice. Very pretty, indeed.

CHARLES. Leonora, I used to go skating with Father on mornings like this. I wish I felt a little better.

(**CHARLES** *rises and starts following* **ERMENGARDE** *toward the right.*)

LEONORA. *(rising)* What! Have I got two invalids on my hands at once? Now, Cousin Ermengarde, you must get better and help me nurse Charles.

ERMENGARDE. I'll do my best.

(**ERMENGARDE** *turns at the very portal and comes back to the table*)

CHARLES. Well, Leonora, I'll do what you ask. I'll write the puppy a letter of forgiveness and apology. It's Christmas Day. I'll cable it. That's what I'll do.

(He goes out the portal right. Slight pause.)

LEONORA. *(drying her eyes)* Ermengarde, it's such a comfort having you here with me. *(Sits in place at left of* **ERMENGARDE,** *formerly occupied by* **GENEVIEVE.**) Mary, I really can't eat anything. Well, perhaps, a sliver of white meat.

ERMENGARDE. *(very old)* I spoke to Mrs. Keene for a moment coming out of church. She asked after the young people. – At church I felt very proud sitting under our windows, Leonora, and our brass tablets. The Bayard aisle – it's a regular Bayard aisle and I love it.

LEONORA. Ermengarde, would you be very angry with me if I went and stayed with the young people a little this spring?

ERMENGARDE. Why, no. I know how badly they want you and need you. Especially now that they're about to build a new house.

LEONORA. You wouldn't be angry? This house is yours as long as you want it, remember.

ERMENGARDE. I don't see why the rest of you dislike it. I like it more than I can say.

LEONORA. I won't be long. I'll be back in no time and we can have some more of our readings aloud in the evening.

(She kisses her and goes into the hall.)

(ERMENGARDE *left alone, eats slowly and talks to Mary)*

ERMENGARDE. Really, Mary, I'll change my mind. If you'll ask Bertha to be good enough to make me a little eggnog. A dear little eggnog. – Such a nice letter this morning from Mrs. Bayard, Mary. Such a nice letter. They're having their first Christmas dinner in the new house. They must be very happy. They call her Mother Bayard, she says, as though she were an old lady. And she says she finds it more comfortable to come and go in a wheelchair. – Such a dear letter…And Mary, I can tell you a secret. It's still a great secret, mind! They're expecting a grandchild. Isn't that good news! Now I'll read a little.

(She props a hook up before her, still dipping a spoon into a custard from time to time. She grows from very old to immensely old. She sighs. She finds a cane beside her, and totters out of the right portal, murmuring:)

Dear little Roderick and little Lucia.

(The audience gazes for a space of time at the table before the lights slowly dim out.)

End of Play

QUEENS OF FRANCE

CHARACTERS

MARIE–SIDONIE CRESSAUX, an attractive young woman.
M'SU CAHUSAC, a lawyer.
MADAME PUGEOT, a plump little bourgeois.
MAMSELLE POINTEVIN, a spinster.
2 extras, **BOY** and **OLD WOMAN.**

SETTING

A lawyer's office in New Orleans, 1869.

(The office door to the street is hung with a reed curtain, through which one obtains a glimpse of a public park in sunshine.)

(A small bell tinkles. After a pause it rings again.)

*(**MARIE-SIDONIE CRESSAUX** pushes the reeds apart and peers in.)*

(She is an attractive young woman equal to any situation in life except a summons to a lawyer's office.)

*(**M'SU CAHUSAC**, a dry little man with sharp black eyes, enters from an inner room.)*

MARIE-SIDONIE. *(indicating a letter in her hand)* You...you have asked me to come and see you.

M. CAHUSAC. *(severe and brief)* Your name, madame?

MARIE-SIDONIE. Mamselle Marie-Sidonie Cressaux, M'su.

M. CAHUSAC. *(after a pause)* Yes. Kindly be seated, Mamselle.

(He goes to his desk and opens a great many drawers, collecting documents from each. Presently having assembled a large bundle, he returns to the center of the room and says abruptly:)

Mamselle, this interview is to be regarded by you as strictly confidential.

MARIE-SIDONIE. Yes , M'su.

M. CAHUSAC. *(after looking at her sternly a moment:)* May I ask if Mamselle is able to bear the shock of surprise, of good or bad news?

MARIE-SIDONIE. Why...yes, M'su.

M. CAHUSAC. Then if you are Mamselle Marie-Sidonie Cressaux, the daughter of Baptiste-Anténor Cressaux, it is my duty to inform you that you are in danger.

MARIE-SIDONIE. I am in danger, M'su?

(He returns to his desk, opens further drawers, and returns with more papers. She follows him with bewildered eyes.)

M. CAHUSAC. Mamselle, in addition to my duties as a lawyer in this city, I am the representative here of a historical society in Paris. Will you please try and follow me, Mamselle? This historical society has been engaged in tracing the descendants of the true heir to the French throne. As you know, at the time of the Revolution, in 1795, to be exact, Mamselle, the true, lawful, and legitimate heir to the French throne disappeared. It was rumored that this boy, who was then ten years old, came to America and lived for a time in New Orleans. We now know that the rumor was true. We now know that he here begot legitimate issue, that this legitimate issue in turn begot legitimate issue, and that –

*(**MARIE-SIDONIE** suddenly starts searching for something in her shopping bag.)*

Mamselle, may I have the honor of your attention a little longer?

MARIE-SIDONIE. *(choking)* My fan – my, my fan, M'su. *(She finds it and at once begins to fan herself wildly. Suddenly she cries out.)* M'su, what danger am I in?

M. CAHUSAC. *(sternly)* If Mamselle will exercise a moment's – one moment's – patience, she will know all…That legitimate issue here begot legitimate issue, and the royal line of France has been traced to a certain *(He consults his documents.)* Baptiste-Anténor Cressaux.

MARIE-SIDONIE. *(Her fan stops and she stares at him.)* Ba't-Ba'tiste!…

M. CAHUSAC. *(leaning forward with menacing emphasis)* Mamselle, can you prove that you are the daughter of Baptiste-Anténor Cressaux?

MARIE-SIDONIE. Why…Why…

M. CAHUSAC. Mamselle, have you a certificate of your parents' marriage?

MARIE-SIDONIE. Yes, M'su.

M. CAHUSAC. If it turns out to be valid, and if it is true that you have no true lawful and legitimate brothers –

MARIE-SIDONIE. No, M'su.

M. CAHUSAC. Then, Mamselle, I have nothing further to do than to announce to you that you are the true and long-lost heir to the throne of France.

> *(He draws himself up, approaches her with great dignity, and kisses her hand.* **MARIE-SIDONIE** *begins to cry. He goes to the desk, pours out a glass of water and, murmuring "Your Royal Highness," offers it to her.)*

MARIE-SIDONIE. M'su Cahusac, I am very sorry...But there must be some mistake. My father was a poor sailor... a...a poor sailor.

M. CAHUSAC. *(reading from his papers)* ...A distinguished and esteemed navigator.

MARIE-SIDONIE. ...A poor sailor...

M. CAHUSAC. *(firmly)* ...Navigator...

> *(Pause.* **MARIE-SIDONIE** *looks about, stricken.)*

MARIE-SIDONIE. *(as before, suddenly and loudly)* M'su, what danger am I in?

M. CAHUSAC. *(approaching her and lowering his voice)* As Your Royal Highness knows, there are several families in New Orleans that claim, without documents *(He rattles the vellum and seals in his hand),* without proof – that pretend to the blood royal. The danger from them, however, is not great. The real danger is from France. From the impassioned Republicans.

MARIE-SIDONIE. Impass...

M. CAHUSAC. But Your Royal Highness has only to put Herself into my hands.

MARIE-SIDONIE. *(crying again)* Please do not call me "Your Royal Highness."

M. CAHUSAC. You...give me permission to call you Madame de Cressaux?

MARIE-SIDONIE. Yes, M'su. Mamselle Cressaux. I am Marie-Sidonie Cressaux.

M. CAHUSAC. Am I mistaken...hmm...in saying that you have children?

MARIE-SIDONIE. *(faintly)* Yes, M'su. I have three children.

(**M. CAHUSAC** *looks at her thoughtfully a moment and returns to his desk.*)

M. CAHUSAC. Madame, from now on thousands of eyes will be fixed upon you, the eyes of the whole world, madame. I cannot urge you too strongly to be very discreet, to be very circumspect.

MARIE-SIDONIE. *(rising, abruptly, nervously)* M'su Cahusac, I do not wish to have anything to do with this. There is a mistake somewhere. I thank you very much, but there is a mistake somewhere. I do not know where. I must go now.

M. CAHUSAC. *(darts forward)* But, Madame, you do not know what you are doing. Your rank cannot be dismissed as easily as that. Do you not know that in a month or two, all the newspapers in the world, including the New Orleans *Times-Picayune*, will publish your name? The first nobles of France will cross the ocean to call upon you. The bishop of Louisiana will call upon you...the mayor...

MARIE-SIDONIE. No, no.

M. CAHUSAC. You will be given a great deal of money and several palaces.

MARIE-SIDONIE. No, no.

M. CAHUSAC. And a guard of soldiers to protect you.

MARIE-SIDONIE. No, no.

M. CAHUSAC. You will be made president of Le Petit Salon and queen of the Mardi Gras...Another sip of water, Your Royal Highness.

MARIE-SIDONIE. Oh, M'su, what shall I do?...Oh, M'su, save me! – I do not want the bishop or the mayor.

M. CAHUSAC. You ask me what you shall do?

MARIE-SIDONIE. Oh, yes, oh, my God!

M. CAHUSAC. For the present, return to your home and lie down. A little rest and a little reflection will tell you what you have to do. Then come and see me Thursday morning.

MARIE-SIDONIE. I think there must be a mistake somewhere.

M. CAHUSAC. May I be permitted to ask Madame de Cressaux a question: Could I have the privilege of presenting Her – until the great announcement takes place – with a small gift of...money?

MARIE-SIDONIE. No, no.

M. CAHUSAC. The historical society is not rich. The historical society has difficulty in pursuing the search for the last documents that will confirm madame's exalted rank, but they would be very happy to advance a certain sum to madame, subscribed by her devoted subjects.

MARIE-SIDONIE. Please no. I do not wish any. I must go now.

M. CAHUSAC. Let me beg madame not to be alarmed. For the present a little rest and reflection...

(The bell rings. He again bends over her hand, murmuring "...obedient servant and devoted subject....")

MARIE-SIDONIE. *(in confusion)* Good-bye, good morning, M. Cahusac. *(She lingers at the door a moment, then returns and says in great earnestness:)* Oh, M. Cahusac, do not let the bishop come and see me. The mayor, yes – but not the bishop.

*(Enter **MADAME PUGEOT**, a plump little bourgeoise in black. Exit **MARIE-SIDONIE**. **M. CAHUSAC** kisses the graciously extended hand of **MADAME PUGEOT**.)*

MME. PUGEOT. Good morning, M. Cahusac.

M. CAHUSAC. Your Royal Highness.

MME. PUGEOT. What business can you possibly be having with that dreadful Marie Cressaux! Do you not know that she is an abandoned woman?

M. CAHUSAC. Alas, we are in the world, Your Royal Highness. For the present I must earn a living as best I can. Mamselle Cressaux is arranging about the purchase of a house and garden.

MME. PUGEOT. Purchase, M. Cahusac, phi! You know very well that she has half a dozen houses and gardens already. She persuades every one of her lovers to give her a little house and garden. She is beginning to own the whole parish of Saint-Magloire.

M. CAHUSAC. Will Your Royal Highness condescend to sit down? *(She does.)* And how is the royal family this morning?

MME. PUGEOT. Only so-so, M'su Cahusac.

M. CAHUSAC. The Archduchess of Tuscany?

MME. PUGEOT. *(fanning herself with a turkey's wing)* A cold. One of her colds. I sometimes think the dear child will never live to see her pearls.

M. CAHUSAC. And the Dauphin, Your Royal Highness?

MME. PUGEOT. Still, still amusing himself in the city, as young men will. Wine, gambling, bad company. At least it keeps him out of harm.

M. CAHUSAC. And the Duke of Burgundy?

MME. PUGEOT. Imagine! The poor child has a sty in his eye!

M. CAHUSAC. Tchk-tchk! *(with solicitude)* In which eye, madame?

MME. PUGEOT. In the left!

M. CAHUSAC. Tchk-tchk! And the Prince of Lorraine and the Duke of Berry?

MME. PUGEOT. They are fairly well, but they seem to mope in their cradle. Their first teeth, my dear chamberlain.

M. CAHUSAC. And your husband, madame?

MME. PUGEOT. *(rises, walks back and forth a moment, then stands still)* From now on we are never to mention him again – while we are discussing these matters. It is to be understood that he is my husband in a manner of speaking only. He has no part in my true life. He has

chosen to scoff at my birth and my rank, but he will see
what he will see...Naturally I have not told him about
the proofs that you and I have collected. I have not the
heart to let him see how unimportant he will become.

M. CAHUSAC. Unimportant, indeed!

MME. PUGEOT. So remember, we do not mention him in
the same breath *with these matters!*

M. CAHUSAC. You must trust me, Madame. *(softly, with sig-
nificance)* And *your* health, Your Royal Highness?

MME. PUGEOT. Oh, very well, thank you. Excellent. I used
to do quite poorly, as you remember, but since this
wonderful news I have been more than well, God be
praised.

M. CAHUSAC. *(as before, with lifted eyebrows)* I beg of you to do
nothing unwise. I beg of you...The little new life we
are all anticipating...

MME. PUGEOT. Have no fear, my dear chamberlain. What is
dear to France is dear to me.

M. CAHUSAC. When I think, madame, of how soon we shall
be able to announce your rank – when I think that this
time next year you will be enjoying all the honors and
privileges that are your due, I am filled with a pious
joy.

MME. PUGEOT. God's will be done, God's will be done.

M. CAHUSAC. At all events, I am particularly happy to see
that Your Royal Highness is in the best of health, for I
have had a piece of disappointing news.

MME. PUGEOT. Chamberlain, you are not going to tell me
that Germany has at last declared war upon my country?

M. CAHUSAC. No, madame.

MME. PUGEOT. You greatly frightened me last week. I could
scarcely sleep. Such burdens as I have! My husband
tells me that I cried out in my sleep the words: *"Paris,
I come!"*

M. CAHUSAC. Sublime, Madame!

MME. PUGEOT. *"Paris, I come,"* like that. I cried out twice in
my sleep: *"Paris, I come."* Oh, these are anxious times;
I am on my way to the cathedral now. This Bismarck
does not understand me. We must avoid a war at all
costs, M. Cahusac...Then what is your news?

M. CAHUSAC. My anxiety at present is more personal. The
historical society in Paris is now confirming the last
proofs of your claim. They have secretaries at work in
all the archives: Madrid, Vienna, Constantinople...

MME. PUGEOT. Constantinople!

M. CAHUSAC. All this requires a good deal of money and
the society is not rich. We have been driven to a painful decision. The society must sell one of the royal
jewels or one of the royal *fournitures* which I am guard-
ing upstairs. The historical society has written me,
Madame, ordering me to send them at once – the
royal christening robe.

MME. PUGEOT. Never!

M. CAHUSAC. The very robe under which Charlemagne was
christened, the Charles, the Henris, the Louis, to lie
under a glass in the Louvre. *(softly)* And this is particularly painful to me because I had hoped – it was, in
fact, the dream of my life – to see at least one of your
children christened under all those fleurs-de-lis.

MME. PUGEOT. It shall not go to the Louvre. I forbid it.

M. CAHUSAC. But what can I do? I offered them the scepter.
I offered them the orb. I even offered them the mug
which Your Royal Highness has already purchased. But
no! The christening robe it must be.

MME. PUGEOT. It shall not leave America! *(clutching her
handbag)* How much are they asking for it?

M. CAHUSAC. Oh, madame, since it is the Ministry of
Museums and Monuments they are asking a great
many thousands of francs.

MME. PUGEOT. And how much would they ask their Queen?

M. CAHUSAC. *(sadly)* Madame, Madame, I cannot see you
purchasing those things which are rightly yours.

MME. PUGEOT. I will purchase it. I shall sell the house on the Chausée Sainte Anne.

M. CAHUSAC. *(softly)* If Your Majesty will give five hundred dollars of Her money I shall add five hundred of my own.

MME. PUGEOT. *(shaken)* Five hundred. Five hundred…Well, you will be repaid many times, my dear chamberlain, when I am restored to my position *(she thinks a moment)* Tomorrow at three. I shall bring you the papers for the sale of the house. You will do everything quietly. My husband will be told about it in due time.

M. CAHUSAC. I understand. I shall be very discreet.

(The bell rings. **M. CAHUSAC** *turns to the door as* **MAMSELLE POINTEVIN** *starts to enter.)*

I shall be free to see you in a few moments, Mamselle. Madame Pugeot has still some details to discuss with me.

MLLE. POINTEVIN. I cannot wait long, M'su Cahusac.

M. CAHUSAC. A few minutes in the park, thank you, Mamselle.

(Exit **MAMSELLE POINTEVIN.** *)*

MME. PUGEOT. Has that poor girl business with a lawyer, M. Cahusac? A poor schoolteacher like that?

M. CAHUSAC. *(softly)* Mamselle Pointevin has taken it into her head to make her will.

MME. PUGEOT. *(laughs superiorly)* Three chairs and a broken plate. *(rising)* Well, tomorrow at three…I am now going to the cathedral. I do not forget the great responsibilities for which I must prepare myself-the army, the navy, the treasury, the appointment of bishops. When I am dead, my dear chamberlain –

M. CAHUSAC. Madame!

MME. PUGEOT. O, no! – even I must die some day…When I am dead, when I am laid with my ancestors, let it never be said of me…By the way, where shall I be laid?

M. CAHUSAC. In the church of Saint Denis, Your Royal Highness?

MME. PUGEOT. Not in Notre Dame?

M. CAHUSAC. No, madame.

MME. PUGEOT. *(meditatively)* Not in Notre Dame. Well *(brightening)* we will cross these bridges when we get to them. *(extending her hand)* Good morning and all my thanks, my dear chamberlain.

M. CAHUSAC. ...Highness's most obedient servant and devoted subject.

MME. PUGEOT. *(beautifully filling the doorway)* Pray for us.

(Exit **MADAME PUGEOT**. **M. CAHUSAC** *goes to the door and bows to* **MAMSELLE POINTEVIN** *in the street.)*

M. CAHUSAC. Now Mamselle, if you will have the goodness to enter.

(Enter **MAMSELLE POINTEVIN**, *a tall and indignant spinster.)*

MLLE. POINTEVIN. M'su Cahusac, it is something new for you to keep me waiting in the public square while you carry on your wretched little business with a vulgar woman like Madame Pugeot. When I condescend to call upon you, my good man, you will have the goodness to receive me at once. Either I am, or I am not, Henriette, Queen of France, Queen of Navarre and Aquitania. It is not fitting that we cool our heels on a public bench among the nursemaids of remote New Orleans. It is hard enough for me to hide myself as a schoolmistress in this city, without having to suffer further humiliations at your hands. Is there no respect due to the blood of Charlemagne?

M. CAHUSAC. Madame...

MLLE. POINTEVIN. Or, sir, are you bored and overfed on the company of queens?

M. CAHUSAC. Madame...

MLLE. POINTEVIN. You are busy with the law. Good! Know, then, La loi-c'est moi. *(sitting down and smoothing out her skirts)* Now what is it you have to say?

M. CAHUSAC. *(pauses a moment, then approaches her with tightly pressed lips and narrowed eyes)* Your Royal Highness, I have received a letter from France. There is some discouraging news.

MLLE. POINTEVIN. No! I cannot afford to buy another thing. I possess the scepter and the orb. Sell the rest to the Louvre, if you must. I can buy them back when my rank is announced.

M. CAHUSAC. Alas!

MLLE. POINTEVIN. What do you mean "alas"?

M. CAHUSAC. Will Your Royal Highness condescend to read the letter I have received from France?

MLLE. POINTEVIN. *(unfurls the letter, but continues looking before her, splendidly)* Have they no bread? Give them cake. *(She starts to read, is shaken, suddenly returns it to him.)* It is too long. It is too long...What does it say?

M. CAHUSAC. It is from the secretary of the historical society. The society remains convinced that you are the true and long-sought heir to the throne of France.

MLLE. POINTEVIN. Convinced? Convinced? I should hope so.

M. CAHUSAC. But to make this conviction public, madame, to announce it throughout the newspapers of the world, including the New Orleans *Times-Picayune*...

MLLE. POINTEVIN. Yes, go on!

M. CAHUSAC. To establish your claim among all your rivals. To establish your claim beyond any possible ridicule...

MLLE. POINTEVIN. Ridicule!

M. CAHUSAC. All they lack is one little document. One little but important document. They had hoped to find it in the archives of Madrid. Madame, it is not there.

MLLE. POINTEVIN. It is not there? Then where is it?

M. CAHUSAC. We do not know, Your Royal Highness. We are in despair.

MLLE. POINTEVIN. Ridicule, M. Cahusac!

(She stares at him, her hand on her mouth.)

M. CAHUSAC. It may be in Constantinople. It may be in Vienna. Naturally we shall continue to search for it. We shall continue to search for generations, for centuries, if need be. But I must confess this is a very discouraging blow.

MLLE. POINTEVIN. Generations! Centuries! But I am not a young girl, M'su Cahusac. Their letter says over and over again that I am the heir to the throne. *(She begins to cry.)*

*(**M. CAHUSAC** discreetly offers her a glass of water.)*

Thank you.

M. CAHUSAC. *(suddenly changing his tone, with firmness)* Madame, you should know that the society suspects the lost document to be in your possession. The society feels sure that the document has been handed down from generation to generation in your family.

MLLE. POINTEVIN. In my possession!

M. CAHUSAC. *(firmly)* Madame, are you concealing something from us?

MLLE. POINTEVIN. Why…no.

M. CAHUSAC. Are you playing with us, as a cat plays with a mouse?

MLLE. POINTEVIN. No indeed I'm not.

M. CAHUSAC. Why is that paper not in Madrid, or in Constantinople or in Vienna? Because it is in your house. You live in what was once your father's house, do you not?

MLLE. POINTEVIN. Yes, I do.

M. CAHUSAC. Go back to it. Look through every old trunk…

MLLE. POINTEVIN. Every old trunk!

M. CAHUSAC. Examine especially the linings. Look through all the tables and desks. Pry into the joints. You will find perhaps a secret drawer, a secret panel.

MLLE. POINTEVIN. M'su Cahusac!

M. CAHUSAC. Examine the walls. Examine the boards of the floor. It may be hidden beneath them.

MLLE. POINTEVIN. I will. I'll go now.

M. CAHUSAC. Have you any old clothes of your father?

MLLE. POINTEVIN. Yes, I have.

M. CAHUSAC. It may be sewn into the lining.

MLLE. POINTEVIN. I'll look.

M. CAHUSAC. Madame, in what suit of clothes was your father buried?

MLLE. POINTEVIN. In his best, M'su.

(She gives a sudden scream under her hand as this thought strikes home. They stare at one another significantly.)

M. CAHUSAC. Take particular pains to look under all steps. These kinds of documents are frequently found under steps. You will find it. If it is not in Madrid, it is there.

MLLE. POINTEVIN. But if I can't find it! *(She sits down, suddenly spent.)* No one will ever know that I am the Queen of France. *(pause)* I am very much afraid, M'su Cahusac, that I shall never find that document in my four rooms. I know every inch of them. But I shall look. *(She draws her hand across her forehead, as though awaking from a dream.)* It is all very strange. You know, M'su Cahusac, I think there may have been a mistake somewhere. It was so beautiful while it lasted. It made even school teaching a pleasure, M'su...And my memoirs. I have just written my memoirs up to the moment when your wonderful announcement came to me – the account of my childhood incognito, the little girl in Louisiana who did not guess the great things before her. But before I go, may I ask something of you? Will you have the historical society write me a letter saying that they seriously think I may be...the person...the person they are looking for? I wish to keep the letter in the trunk with the orb and...with the scepter. You know...the more I think of it, the more I think there must have been a mistake somewhere.

M. CAHUSAC. The very letter you have in mind is here, madame.

(He gives it to her.)

MLLE. POINTEVIN. Thank you. And M'su Cahusac, may I ask another favor of you?

M. CAHUSAC. Certainly, madame.

MLLE. POINTEVIN. Please, never mention this...this whole affair to anyone in New Orleans.

M. CAHUSAC. Madame, not unless you wish it.

MLLE. POINTEVIN. Good morning – good morning, and thank you. *(Her handkerchief to one eye, she goes out.)*

*(**M. CAHUSAC** goes to his desk.)*

*(The bell rings. The reed curtain is parted and a **NEGRO BOY** pushes in a wheelchair containing a **WOMAN** of some hundred years of age. She is wrapped in shawls, like a mummy, and wears a scarf about her head, and green spectacles on her nose. The mummy extends a hand which **M. CAHUSAC** kisses devotedly, murmuring, "Your Royal Highness.")*

End of Play

PULLMAN CAR HIAWATHA

CHARACTERS

THE STAGE MANAGER

Compartment Three: **AN INSANE WOMAN**, *Mrs. Churchill*
MALE ATTENDANT, *Mr. Morgan*
THE FEMALE ATTENDANT, *A trained nurse*

Compartment Two: **PHILIP MILBURY**

Compartment Three: **HARRIET MILBURY**, *Philip's young wife*

Lower One: **A MAIDEN LADY**

Lower Three: **A MIDDLE-AGED DOCTOR**

Lower Five: **A STOUT, AMIABLE WOMAN**

Lower Seven: **AN ENGINEER**, <u>*Bill*</u>*, going to California*

Lower Nine: **AN ENGINEER**, *Fred*
THE PORTER, *Harrison*
GROVER'S CORNERS, OHIO, *represented by a Grinning Boy*
THE FIELD, *represented by Somebody in Shirt Sleeves*
A TRAMP
PARKERSBURG, OHIO, *represented by a Farmer's Wife and Three Young People*
A WORKMAN, *Mr. Krüger, a ghost*
THE WORKER, *a watchman*
THE WEATHER, *represented by a Mechanic*

The Hours: **TEN O'CLOCK**
ELEVEN O'CLOCK   *represented by*
TWELVE O'CLOCK   *Three Beautiful Women*

The Planets: **SATURN**
VENUS
JUPITER
EARTH

The Archangels: **GABRIEL**
MICHAEL

SETTING

A Pullman car making its way from New York to Chicago, December 1930.

(At the back of the stage is a balcony or bridge or runway leading out of sight in both directions. Two flights of stairs descend from it to the stage. There is no further scenery.)

(At the rise of the curtain **THE STAGE MANAGER** *is making lines with a piece of chalk on the floor of the stage by the footlights.)*

THE STAGE MANAGER. This is the plan of a Pullman car. Its name is *Hiawatha* and on December twenty-first it is on its way from New York to Chicago. Here at your left are three compartments. Here is the aisle and five lowers. The berths are all full, uppers and lowers, but for the purposes of this play we are limiting our interest to the people in the lower berths on the further side only. The berths are already made-up. It is half past nine. Most of the passengers are in bed behind the green curtains. They are dropping their shoes on the floor, or wrestling with their trousers, or wondering whether they dare hide their valuables in the pillow slips during the night. All right! Come on, everybody!

(The actors enter carrying chairs. Each improvises his berth by placing two chairs "facing one another" in his chalk-marked space. They then sit in one chair, profile to the audience, and rest their feet on the other. This must do for lying in bed. The passengers in the compartments do the same. Reading from Left to Right we have: Compartment Three. Compartment Two, Compartment One, Lower One, Lower Three, Lower Five, Lower Seven, Lower Nine.)

LOWER ONE. Porter, be sure and wake me up at quarter of six.

THE PORTER. Yes, ma'am.

LOWER ONE. I know I shan't sleep a wink, but I want to be told when it's quarter of six.

THE PORTER. Yes, ma'am.

 LOWER SEVEN. *(putting his head through the curtains)* Hsst! Porter! Hsst! How the hell do you turn on this other light?

THE PORTER. *(fussing with it)* I'm afraid it's outta order, suh. You'll have to use the other end.

THE STAGE MANAGER. *(falsetto, substituting for some woman in an upper berth)* May I ask if someone in this car will be kind enough to lend me some aspirin?

THE PORTER. *(rushing about)* Yes, ma'am.

LOWER NINE. *(one of the engineers, descending the aisle and falling into Lower Five)* Sorry, lady, sorry. Made a mistake.

LOWER FIVE. *(grumbling)* Never in all my born days!

LOWER ONE. *(in a shrill whisper)* Porter! Porter!

THE PORTER. Yes, ma'am.

LOWER ONE. My hot water bag's leaking. I guess you'll have to take it away. I'll have to do without it tonight. How awful!

LOWER FIVE. *(sharply to the passenger above her)* Young man, you mind your own business, or I'll report you to the conductor.

THE STAGE MANAGER. *(substituting for Upper Five)* Sorry, ma'am, I didn't mean to upset you. My suspenders fell down and I was trying to catch them.

LOWER FIVE. Well, here they are. Now go to sleep. Everybody seems to be rushing into my berth tonight. *(She puts her head out.)* Porter! Porter! Be a good soul and bring me a glass of water, will you? I'm parched.

LOWER NINE. Bill!

(no answer)

Bill!

 LOWER SEVEN. Yea? Wha'd'ya want?

LOWER NINE. Slip me one of those magazines, willya?

 LOWER SEVEN. Which one d'ya want?

LOWER NINE. Either one. *Detective Stories.* Either one.

LOWER SEVEN. Aw, Fred. I'm just in the middle of one of
'em in *Detective Stories.*

LOWER NINE. That's all right. I'll take the *Western.* – Thanks.

THE STAGE MANAGER. *(to the actors)* All right! – Sh! Sh! Sh!
(to the audience) Now I want you to hear them thinking.

*(There is a pause and then they all begin a murmuring-
swishing noise, very soft. In turn each one of them can
be heard above the others.)*   Atmosphere → murmur

LOWER FIVE. *(The Woman of Fifty)* Let's see, I've got the
doll for the baby. And the slip-on for Marietta. And
the fountain pen for Herbert. And the subscription to
Time for George…

LOWER SEVEN. *(Bill)* God! Lillian, if you don't turn out to
be what I think you are, I don't know what I'll do. – I
guess it's bad politics to let a woman know that you're
going all the way to California to see her. I'll think up
a song-and-dance about a business trip or something.
Was I ever as hot and bothered about anyone like this
before? Well, there was Martha. But that was different. I'd better try and read or I'll go cuckoo. "How did
you know it was ten o'clock when the visitor left the
house?" asked the detective. "Because at ten o'clock,"
answered the girl, "I always turn out the lights in the
conservatory and in the back hall. As I was coming
down the stairs I heard the master talking to someone at the front door. I heard him say, 'Well, good
night…'" – Gee, I don't feel like reading; I'll just think
about Lillian. That yellow hair. Them eyes!…

LOWER THREE. *(The Doctor reads aloud to himself the most hair-
raising material from a medical journal, every now and then
punctuating his reading with an interrogative "So?")*

LOWER ONE. *(The Maiden Lady)* I know I'll be awake all
night. I might just as well make up my mind to it now.
I can't imagine what got hold of that hot water bag to
leak on the train of all places. Well now, I'll lie on my
right side and breathe deeply and think of beautiful
things, and perhaps I can doze off a bit.

(And lastly:)

LOWER NINE. *(Fred)* That was the craziest thing I ever did. It's set me back three whole years. I could have saved up thirty thousand dollars by now, if I'd only stayed over here. What business had I got to fool with contracts with the goddam Soviets. Hell, I thought it would be interesting. Interesting, what the hell! It's set me back three whole years. I don't even know if the company'll take me back. I'm green, that's all. I just don't grow up.

(**THE STAGE MANAGER** *strides toward them with lifted hand, crying, "Hush," and their whispering ceases.*)

THE STAGE MANAGER. That'll do! – Just one minute. Porter!

THE PORTER. *(appearing at the left)* Yessuh.

THE STAGE MANAGER. It's your turn to think. (**THE PORTER** *is very embarrassed*). Don't you want to? You have a right to.

THE PORTER. *(torn between the desire to release his thoughts and his shyness)* Ah…ah…I'm only thinkin' about my home in Chicago and…and my life insurance.

THE STAGE MANAGER. That's right.

THE PORTER. …Well, thank you…Thank you.

(**THE PORTER** *slips away, blushing violently, in an agony of self-consciousness and pleasure.*)

THE STAGE MANAGER. *(to the audience)* He's a good fellow, Harrison is. Just shy.

(to the actors again) Now the compartments, please.

(The berths fall into shadow. **PHILIP** *is standing at the door connecting his compartment with his wife's.)*

PHILIP. Are you all right, angel?

HARRIET. Yes. I don't know what was the matter with me during dinner.

PHILIP. Shall I close the door?

HARRIET. Do see whether you can't put a chair against it that will hold it half open without banging.

PHILIP. There. – Good night, angel. If you can't sleep, call me and we'll sit up and play Russian Bank.

HARRIET. You're thinking of that awful time when we sat up every night for a week...But at least I know I shall sleep tonight. The noise of the wheels has become sort of nice and homely. What state are we in?

PHILIP. We're tearing through Ohio. We'll be in Indiana soon.

HARRIET. I know those little towns full of horse blocks.

PHILIP. Well, we'll reach Chicago very early. I'll call you. Sleep tight.

HARRIET. Sleep tight, darling.

> (**PHILIP** *returns to his own compartment. In Compartment Three, the* **MALE ATTENDANT** *tips his chair back against the wall and smokes a cigar. The* **TRAINED NURSE** *knits a stocking. The* **INSANE WOMAN** *leans her forehead against the windowpane, that is, stares into the audience.*)

THE INSANE WOMAN. *(Her words have a dragging, complaining sound, but lack any conviction.)* Don't take me there. Don't take me there.

THE FEMALE ATTENDANT. Wouldn't you like to lie down, dearie?

THE INSANE WOMAN. I want to get off the train. I want to go back to New York.

THE FEMALE ATTENDANT. Wouldn't you like me to brush your hair again? It's such a nice feeling.

THE INSANE WOMAN. *(going to the door)* I want to get off the train. I want to open the door.

THE FEMALE ATTENDANT. *(taking one of her hands)* Such a noise! You'll wake up all the nice people. Come and I'll tell you a story about the place we're going to.

THE INSANE WOMAN. I don't want to go to that place.

THE FEMALE ATTENDANT. Oh, it's lovely! There are lawns and gardens everywhere. I never saw such a lovely place. Just lovely.

THE INSANE WOMAN. *(lies down on the bed)* Are there roses?

THE FEMALE ATTENDANT. Roses! Red, yellow, white…just everywhere.

THE MALE ATTENDANT. *(after a pause)* That musta been Cleveland.

THE FEMALE ATTENDANT. I had a case in Cleveland once. Diabetes.

THE MALE ATTENDANT. *(after another pause)* I wisht I had a radio here. Radios are good for *them*. I had a patient once that had to have the radio going every minute.

THE FEMALE ATTENDANT. Radios are lovely. My married niece has one. It's always going. It's wonderful.

THE INSANE WOMAN. *(half rising)* I'm not beautiful. I'm not beautiful as she was.

THE FEMALE ATTENDANT. Oh, I think you're beautiful! Beautiful. – Mr. Morgan, don't you think Mrs. Churchill is beautiful?

THE MALE ATTENDANT. Oh, fine lookin'! Regular movie star, Mrs. Churchill.

(**THE INSANE WOMAN** *looks inquiringly at them and subsides.* **HARRIET** *groans slightly. Smothers a cough. She gropes about with her hand and finds the bell.* **THE PORTER** *knocks at her door.*)

HARRIET. *(whispering)* Come in. First, please close the door into my husband's room. Softly. Softly.

THE PORTER. *(a plaintive porter)* Yes, ma'am.

HARRIET. Porter, I'm not well. I'm sick. I must see a doctor.

THE PORTER. Why ma'am, they ain't no doctor…

HARRIET. Yes, when I was coming out from dinner I saw a man in one of the seats on that side, reading medical papers. Go and wake him up.

THE PORTER. *(flabbergasted)* Ma'am, I cain't wake anybody up.

HARRIET. Yes, you can. Porter. Porter. Now don't argue with me. I'm very sick. It's my heart. Wake him up. Tell him it's my heart.

THE PORTER. Yes, ma'am.

(He goes into the aisle and starts pulling the shoulder of the man in Lower Three.)

LOWER THREE. Hello. Hello. What is it? Are we there?

*(***THE PORTER*** mumbles to him.)*

I'll be right there. – Porter, is it a young woman or an old one?

THE PORTER. I dunno, suh. I guess she's kinda old, suh, but not so very old.

LOWER THREE. Tell her I'll be there in a minute and to lie quietly.

*(***THE PORTER*** enters ***HARRIET***'s compartment. She has turned her head away.)*

THE PORTER. He'll be here in a minute, ma'am. He says you lie quiet.

*(***LOWER THREE*** stumbles along the aisle muttering "Damn these shoes!")*

SOMEONE'S VOICE. Can't we have a little quiet in this car, please?

LOWER NINE. *(Fred)* Oh, shut up!

*(***LOWER THREE*** [The Doctor] passes ***THE PORTER*** and enters ***HARRIET***'s compartment. He leans over her, concealing her by his stooping figure)*

LOWER THREE. She's dead, Porter. Is there anyone on the train traveling with her?

THE PORTER. Yessuh. Dat's her husband in dere.

LOWER THREE. Idiot! Why didn't you call him? I'll go in and speak to him.

*(***THE STAGE MANAGER*** comes forward.)*

THE STAGE MANAGER. All right. So much for the inside of the car. That'll be enough of that for the present. Now for its position geographically, meteorologically, astronomically, theologically considered.

Pullman Car Hiawatha, ten minutes of ten. December twenty-first, 1930. All ready.

(Some figures begin to appear on the balcony.)

THE STAGE MANAGER. No, no. It's not time for The Planets yet. Nor The Hours.

(They retire.)

*(***THE STAGE MANAGER*** *claps his hands. A Grinning Boy in overalls enters from the left behind the berths.)*

GROVER'S CORNERS, OHIO. *(in a foolish voice as though he were reciting a piece at a Sunday school entertainment)* I represent Grover's Corners, Ohio. Eight hundred twenty-one souls. "There's so much good in the worst of us and so much bad in the best of us, that it ill behooves any of us to criticize the rest of us." Robert Louis Stevenson. Thankya.

(He grins and goes out right. Enter from the same direction Somebody in Shirt Sleeves. This is a field.)

THE FIELD. I represent a field you are passing between Grover's Corners, Ohio, and Parkersburg, Ohio. In this field there are fifty-one gophers, two hundred and six field mice, six snakes and millions of bugs, insects, ants and spiders. All in their winter sleep. "What is so rare as a day in June? Then, if ever, come perfect days." The Vision of Sir Launfal, William Cullen – I mean James Russell Lowell. Thank you.

(Exit. Enter a tramp.)

THE TRAMP. I just want to tell you that I'm a tramp that's been traveling under this car, Hiawatha, so I have a right to be in this play. I'm going from Rochester, New York, to Joliet, Illinois. It takes a lotta people to make a world. "On the road to Mandalay, where the flying fishes play and the sun comes up like thunder, over China, 'cross the bay." Frank W. Service. It's bitter cold. Thank you.

(Exit. Enter a gentle old farmer's wife with three stringy young people.)

PARKERSBURG, OHIO. I represent Parkersburg, Ohio. Twenty-six hundred and four souls. I have seen all the dreadful havoc that alcohol has done and I hope no one here will ever touch a drop of the curse of this beautiful country.

(She heats a measure and they all sing unsteadily:)

"Throw out the lifeline! Throw out the lifeline! Someone is sinking today-ay…"

(THE STAGE MANAGER *waves them away tactfully. Enter a workman.)*

THE WORKMAN. Ich bin der Arbeiter der hier sein Leben verlor. Bei der Sprengung für diese Brücke über die Sie in dem Moment fahren –

(The engine whistles for a trestle crossing.)

– erschlug mich ein Felsblock. Ich spiele jetzt als Geist in diesem Stück mit. "Vor sieben und achtzig Jahren haben unsere Väter auf diesem Kontinent eine neue Nation hervorgebracht…"

THE STAGE MANAGER. *(helpfully, to the audience)* I'm sorry; that's in German. He says that he's the ghost of a workman who was killed while they were building the trestle over which the car Hiawatha is now passing

(The engine whistles again.)

– and he wants to appear in this play. A chunk of rock hit him while they were dynamiting. – His motto you know: "Three score and seven years ago our fathers brought forth upon this continent a new nation dedicated…" and so on. Thank you, Mr. Krüger.

(Exit the ghost. Enter another worker.)

THE WORKER. I'm a watchman in a tower near Parkersburg, Ohio. I just want to tell you that I'm not asleep and that the signals are all right for this train. I hope you all have a fine trip. "If you can keep your head when all about you are losing theirs and blaming it on you…" Rudyard Kipling. Thank you.

(He exits. **THE STAGE MANAGER** *comes forward.)*

THE STAGE MANAGER. All right. That'll be enough of that. Now the weather.

(Enter a **MECHANIC.***)*

A MECHANIC. It is eleven degrees above zero. The wind is north-northwest, velocity fifty-seven. There is a field of low barometric pressure moving eastward from Saskatchewan to the eastern coast. Tomorrow it will be cold with some snow in the middle western states and northern New York.

(He exits.)

THE STAGE MANAGER. All right. Now for The Hours.
(helpfully to the audience) The minutes are gossips; the hours are philosophers; the years are theologians. The hours are philosophers with the exception of Twelve O' clock who is also a theologian. – Ready Ten O'clock!

(THE HOURS *are beautiful girls dressed like Elihu Vedder's Pleiades. Each carries a great gold Roman numeral. They pass slowly across the balcony at the back, moving from right to left.)*

What are you doing, Ten O'clock? Aristotle?

TEN O'CLOCK. No, Plato, Mr. Washburn.

THE STAGE MANAGER. Good. – "Are you not rather convinced that he who thus…"

TEN O'CLOCK. "Are you not rather convinced that he who thus sees Beauty as only it can be seen will be specially favored? And since he is in contact not with images but with realities…" *(She continues the passage in a murmur as* **ELEVEN O'CLOCK** *appears.)*

ELEVEN O'CLOCK. "What else can I, Epictetus, do, a lame old man, but sing hymns to God? If then I were a nightingale, I would do the nightingale's part. If I were a swan, I would do a swan's. But now I am a rational creature…" *(Her voice also subsides to a murmur.* **TWELVE O'CLOCK** *appears.)*

THE STAGE MANAGER. Good. – Twelve O'clock, what have you?

TWELVE O'CLOCK. Saint Augustine and his mother.

THE STAGE MANAGER. So. – "And we began to say: If to any the tumult of the flesh were hushed…"

TWELVE O'CLOCK. "And we began to say: If to any the tumult of the flesh were hushed; hushed the images of earth; of waters and of air…"

THE STAGE MANAGER. Faster. – "Hushed also the poles of Heaven."

TWELVE O'CLOCK. "Yea, were the very soul to be hushed to herself."

THE STAGE MANAGER. A little louder, Miss Foster.

TWELVE O'CLOCK. *(a little louder)* "Hushed all dreams and imaginary revelations…"

THE STAGE MANAGER. *(waving them back)* All right. All right. Now The Planets. December twenty-first, 1930, please.

*(**THE HOURS** unwind and return to their dressing rooms at the right. **THE PLANETS** appear on the balcony. Some of them take their place halfway on the steps. These have no words, but each has a sound. One has a pulsating, zinging sound. Another has a thrum. One whistles ascending and descending scales. Saturn does a slow, obstinate humming sound on two repeated low notes.)*

Louder, Saturn. – Venus, higher. Good. Now, Jupiter. – Now the Earth.

*(**THE STAGE MANAGER** turns to the beds on the train.)*

Come, everybody. This is the Earth's sound.

(The towns, workmen, etc., appear at the edge of the stage. The passengers begin their "thinking" murmur.)

Come, Grover's Corners. Parkersburg. You're in this. Watchman. Tramp. This is the Earth's sound.

*(He conducts it as the director of an orchestra would. Each of the towns and workmen does his motto. **THE INSANE WOMAN** breaks into passionate weeping. She rises and stretches out her arms to **THE STAGE MANAGER**.)*

THE INSANE WOMAN. Use me. Give me something to do.

(He goes to her quickly, whispers something in her ear, and leads her back to her guardians. She is unconsoled.)

THE STAGE MANAGER. Now shh-shh-shh! Enter The Archangels.

(to the audience) We have now reached the theological position of Pullman Car Hiawatha.

(The towns and workmen have disappeared. The Planets, offstage, continue a faint music. Two young men in blue serge suits enter along the balcony and descend the stairs at the right. As they pass each bed the passenger talks in his sleep.)

*(**GABRIEL** points out Bill to **MICHAEL** who smiles with raised eyebrows. They pause before Lower Five, and **MICHAEL** makes the sound of assent that can only be rendered "Hn-Hn.")*

(The remarks that the characters make in their sleep are not all intelligible, being lost in the sound of sigh or groan or whisper by which they are conveyed. But we seem to hear:)

LOWER NINE. *(loud)* Some people are slower than others, that's all.

LOWER SEVEN. *(Bill)* It's no fun, y'know. I'll try.

LOWER FIVE. *(the lady of the Christmas presents, rapidly)* You know best, of course. I'm ready whenever you are. One year's like another.

LOWER ONE. I can teach sewing. I can sew.

*(They approach **HARRIET**'s compartment. **THE INSANE WOMAN** sits up and speaks to them.)*

THE INSANE WOMAN. Me?

*(The **ARCHANGELS** shake their heads.)*

What possible use can there be in my simply waiting? – Well, I'm grateful for anything. I'm grateful for being so much better than I was. The old story, the terrible story, doesn't haunt me as it used to. A great load seems to have been taken off my mind. – But no one understands me any more. At last I understand myself perfectly, but no one else understands a thing I say. – So I must wait?

(*The* **ARCHANGELS** *nod, smiling.*)

(*resignedly, and with a smile that implies their complicity:*)

THE INSANE WOMAN. (*cont.*) Well, you know best. I'll do whatever is best; but everyone is so childish, so absurd. They have no logic. These people are all so mad... These people are like children; they have never suffered.

(*She returns to her bed and sleeps. The* **ARCHANGELS** *stand beside* **HARRIET.** *The* **DOCTOR** *has drawn* **PHILIP** *into the next compartment and is talking to him in earnest whispers.* **HARRIET**'s *face has been toward the wall; she turns it slightly and speaks toward the ceiling.*)

HARRIET. I wouldn't be happy there. Let me stay dead down here. I belong here. I shall be perfectly happy to roam about my house and be near Philip. – You know I wouldn't be happy there.

(**GABRIEL** *leans over and whispers into her ear. After a short pause she bursts into fierce tears.*)

I'm ashamed to come with you. I haven't done anything. I haven't done anything with my life. Worse than that I was angry and sullen. I never realized anything. I don't dare go a step in such a place.

(*They whisper to her again.*)

But it's not possible to forgive such things. I don't want to be forgiven so easily. I want to be punished for it all. I won't stir until I've been punished a long, long time. I want to be freed of all that – by punishment. I want to be all new.

(*They whisper to her. She puts her feet slowly on the ground.*)

HARRIET. *(cont.)* But no one else could be punished for me. I'm willing to face it all myself. I don't ask anyone to be punished for me.

(They whisper to her again. She sits long and brokenly looking at her shoes, thinking it over.)

It wasn't fair. I'd have been willing to suffer for it myself – if I could have endured such a mountain.

(She smiles) Oh, I'm ashamed! I'm just a stupid and you know it. I'm just another American. – But then what wonderful things must be beginning now. You really want me? You really want me?

(They start leading her down the aisle of the car.)

Let's take the whole train. There are some lovely faces on this train. Can't we all come? You'll never find anyone better than Philip. Please, please, let's all go.

*(They reach the steps. The **ARCHANGELS** interlock their arms as a support for her as she leans heavily on them, taking the steps slowly. Her words are half singing and half babbling.)*

But look at how tremendously high and far it is. I've a weak heart. I'm not supposed to climb stairs. "I do not ask to see the distant scene: One step enough for me." It's like Switzerland. My tongue keeps saying things. I can't control it. – Do let me stop a minute: I want to say good-bye.

(She turns in their arms.)

Just a minute, I want to cry on your shoulder.

*(She leans her forehead against **GABRIEL**'s shoulder and laughs long and softly.)*

Good-bye, Philip. – I begged him not to marry me, but he would. He believed in me just as you do. – Goodbye, 1312 Ridgewood Avenue, Oaksbury, Illinois. I hope I remember all its steps and doors and wall-papers forever. Good-bye, Emerson Grammar School on the corner of Forbush Avenue and Wherry Street.

Good-bye, Miss Walker and Miss Cramer who taught
me English and Miss Matthewson who taught me biol-
ogy. Good-bye, First Congregational Church on the
corner of Meyerson Avenue and Sixth Street and Dr.
McReady and Mrs. McReady and Julia. Good-bye, Papa
and Mama…

(She turns.)

HARRIET. *(cont.)* Now I'm tired of saying good-bye. – I never
used to talk like this. I was so homely I never used to
have the courage to talk. Until Philip came. I see now.
I see now. I understand everything now.

*(**THE STAGE MANAGER** comes forward.)*

THE STAGE MANAGER. *(to the actors)* All right. All right. –
Now we'll have the whole world together, please. The
whole solar system, please.

*(The complete cast begins to appear at the edges of the
stage. He claps his hands.)*

The whole solar system, please. Where's The Tramp? –
Where's The Moon?

*(He gives two raps on the floor, like the conductor of
an orchestra attracting the attention of his forces, and
slowly lifts his hand. The human beings murmur their
thoughts; The Hours discourse; The Planets chant
or hum. **HARRIET**'s voice finally rises above them all,
saying.)*

HARRIET. "I was not ever thus, nor asked that Thou
Shouldst lead me on, and spite of fears,
Pride ruled my will: Remember not past years."

*(**THE STAGE MANAGER** waves them away.)*

THE STAGE MANAGER. Very good. Now clear the stage,
please. Now we're at Englewood Station, South
Chicago. See the university's towers over there! The
best of them all.

LOWER ONE. *(The Maiden Lady)* Porter, you promised to
wake me up at quarter of six.

THE PORTER. Sorry, ma'am, but it's been an awful night on this car. A lady's been terrible sick.

LOWER ONE. Oh! Is she better?

THE PORTER. N o'm. She ain't one jot better.

LOWER FIVE. Young man, take your foot out of my face.

THE STAGE MANAGER. *(again substituting for Upper Five)* Sorry, lady, I slipped –

LOWER FIVE. *(grumbling not unamiably)* I declare, this trip's been one long series of insults.

THE STAGE MANAGER. Just one minute, ma'am, and I'll be down and out of your way.

LOWER FIVE. Haven't you got anybody to darn your socks for you? You ought to be ashamed to go about that way.

THE STAGE MANAGER. Sorry, lady.

LOWER FIVE. You're too stuck up to get married. That's the trouble with you.

LOWER NINE. Bill! Bill!

LOWER SEVEN. Yea? Wha'd'ya want?

LOWER NINE. Bill, how much d'ya give the porter on a train like this? I've been outta the country so long…

LOWER SEVEN. Hell, Fred, I don't know myself.

THE PORTER. CHICAGO, CHICAGO. All out. This train don't go no further.

(The passengers jostle their way out and an army of old women with mops and pails enter and prepare to clean up the car.)

End of Play

LOVE AND HOW TO CURE IT

CHARACTERS

LINDA, a dancer, sixteen
JOEY WESTON, a comedian
ROWENA STOKER, a comedic actress and singer, Linda's aunt
ARTHUR WARBURTON, Linda's admirer

SETTING

The stage of the Tivoli Palace of Music, Soho, London, April 1895.

(The stage is dark save for a gas jet forward left and an oil lamp on the table at the back right.)

(bare, dark, dusty and cold)

*(**LINDA**, dressed in a white ballet dress, is practicing steps and bending exercises. She is a beautiful, impersonal, remote, almost sullen girl of barely sixteen.)*

*(At the table in the distance sit **JOEY**, a stout comedian, and **ROWENA**, a mature soubrette. **JOEY** is reading aloud from a pink theatrical and sporting weekly and **ROWENA** is darning a stocking. When they speak the touch of cockney in their diction is insufficiently compensated by touches of exaggerated elegance. There is silence for a time, broken only by the undertone of the reading and the whispered counting of **LINDA** at her practice. Then:)*

ROWENA. *(calling to **LINDA**)* They've put off the rehearsal. Mark my words. It's after half past eight now. They must have got word to the others somehow. Or else we understood the day wrong. – Go on, Joey.

*(**JOEY** reads for a few minutes, then **ROWENA** calls again.)*

Linda, the paper says Marjorie FitzMaurice has an engagement. An Ali Baba and the Forty Thieves company that Moss has collected for Folkstone, Brighton and the piers. She must have got better. – You'd better take a rest, dearie. You'll be all blowed. – Go on, Joey, that's a good boy.

LINDA. *(gravely describing an arc waist-high with her toe)* It's nine o'clock. I can hear the chimes.

*(Apparently **JOEY** has finished the paper. He stretches and yawns. **ROWENA** puts down her work, picks up her chair and brings it toward the footlights, and starts firmly supervising **LINDA**'s movements.)*

ROWENA. One, two, three; one, two, three. Whatever are you doing with your hands, child? Madame Angellelli didn't teach you anything like that. Bend them back like you was discovering a flower by surprise. That's right. – Upsidaisy! That's the way. – Now that's enough kicks for one night. If you must do any more, just stick to the knee-highs.

(She yawns and pats her yawn.)

There's no rehearsal. We might just as well go home. It was all a mistake somehow.

LINDA. *(almost upside down)* No, no. I don't want to go home. Besides, I'm hungry. Ask Joey to go around the corner and buy some fish and chips.

ROWENA. Goodness, I never saw such an eater. Well, I have two kippers here I was going to set on for breakfast. *(calling)* Joey, there's a stove downstairs still, isn't there?

JOEY. Yes.

ROWENA. *(to* **LINDA***)* There you are! We could have a little supper and ask Joey. I have a packet of tea in my bag. How would you like that, angel?

LINDA. Lovely.

ROWENA. Joey, how would you like a little supper on the stage with kipper and tea and everything nice?

JOEY. Like it! I'm that starved I could eat bones and all. Wot's more, I'll cook it for you. I'm the best little cooker of a kipper for a copper you could 'ope to see.

ROWENA. *(meditatively)* You could use that in a song some-day, Joey. – Shall I let him cook it, Linda?

LINDA. Yes, let him cook it.

JOEY. I'll just go next door and get a spoonful of butter.

ROWENA. There's sixpence. Get some milk for the tea, too. Put some water on as you go out and I'll be down in a minute to make the tea.

JOEY. Won't be a minute, my dears.

(He hurries out. There is a pause. **LINDA** *stops her exercise and examines attentively each of the soles of her slippers in turn.)*

ROWENA. Joey must have cooked thousands of kippers in his day. All those last years when his wife was ill, he cooked everything for her. Good old Joey! He's all lost without her. And he wants me to talk about her all the time, only he doesn't want to bring her into the conversation first. You know, Henrietta du Vaux was wonderful, but I can't talk about her forever.

(another pause)

Linda, whatever are you thinking about all the time?

LINDA. Nothing.

ROWENA. Don't you say "Nothing." Come now, tell your auntie. What is it you keep turning over in your mind all the time?

LINDA. *(indifferently)* Well, almost nothing – except that I'm going to be shot any minute.

ROWENA. Don't say such things, dearie. No one's going to shoot you. You ought to be ashamed to say such things.

LINDA. *(pointing scornfully to the door)* He's out waiting in the street this very minute.

ROWENA. Why, he went back to his university didn't he? He's a student. They don't let them come to London whenever they want.

LINDA. Oh, I don't care! Let him shoot me. I wish I'd never seen him. What was he doing, anyway – worming his way into Madame Angellelli's soirees. He'd oughta stayed among his own people.

ROWENA. I'm going out into the street this minute to see if he's there. I can get the police after him for hounding a poor girl so. What's his name?

LINDA. Arthur Warburton. I tell you I don't care if he shoots me.

ROWENA. *(sharply)* Now I won't have you saying things like that! Now mind! If he's out there Joey'll go and get him and we'll have a talk. When did you see him last?

LINDA. Sunday. We had tea at Richmond and went boating on the river.

ROWENA. Did you let him kiss you?

LINDA. I let him kiss me once when we floated under some willow trees. And then he kept talking so hotheaded that I didn't let him kiss me again, and I liked him less and less. All the way back on the bus, I didn't pay any attention to him; just looked into the street and said yes and no; and then I told him I was too busy to see him this week. I don't want to see him again. – Aunt Rowena, he breathes so hard.

ROWENA. He didn't look like he was rough and nasty.

LINDA. He's not rough and nasty. He just...suffers.

ROWENA. I know 'em.

LINDA. Aunt Rowena, isn't there any way discovered to make a man get over loving you. Can it be cured?

*(**ROWENA** does not answer. She walks meditatively back to the table in the corner.)*

ROWENA. Give me a hand, will you, with this table. We'll bring it nearer to the gas jet. I'd better go downstairs and see what Joey's doing to everything. *(They bring the table forward.)* Dearie, what makes you say such things? What makes you say he's thinking of shooting you?

LINDA. He looked all...all crazy and said I oughtn't to be alive. He said if I didn't marry him...

ROWENA. Marry him! He asked you to marry him? Linda, you are a funny girl not to tell me these things before. Why do you keep everything so secret, dearie?

LINDA. I didn't think that was a secret. I don't want to marry him.

ROWENA. *(passing her thumb along her teeth and looking at* **LINDA** *narrowly)* Well, now try and remember what he said about shooting.

LINDA. He was standing at the door saying good-bye. I was playing with the key in my hand to show him I was in a hurry to be done with him. He said he couldn't think of anything but me – that he couldn't live without me and so on. Then he asked me was there someone else I loved instead of him, and I said no. And he said how about the Italian fellow at Madame Angellelli's soiree, and I said no, not in a thousand years. He meant Mario. And then he started to cry and take on terrible. – Imagine being jealous of Mario.

ROWENA. I'll teach that young man a lesson. That's what I'll do.

LINDA. Then he was trembling all over, and he took up the edge of my coat and cried: People like me ought not to be alive. Nature ought not to allow such soulless beauties like I.

*(**LINDA** has risen on her toes, holding out her arms, and has started drifting away with little rapid steps. From the back of the stage she calls scornfully.)*

I ought not to be alive, he said. I ought not to be alive.

(pause)

ROWENA. Someone's pounding on the street door down there. Joey must have dropped the latch.

LINDA. It's Arthur.

ROWENA. Don't be foolish.

LINDA. I know in my bones it's him.

*(**JOEY** appears at the back.)*

JOEY. There's a gentleman to see you, Linda. Says his name is Warburton.

LINDA. Yes. Send him up.

JOEY. Kipper is almost ready. Water's boiling, Rowena. What are you going to do about this visitor?

ROWENA. Listen, dearie, I want to look at this Arthur again. You ask him pretty to have supper with us.

LINDA. Oh, Aunt Rowena, I couldn't eat!

ROWENA. This is serious. This is serious, Linda. Now you ask him to supper and send him around the corner for some bitters. In the meantime I'll catch a minute to tell Joey how we must watch him.

LINDA. I don't care if he shoots me. It's nothing to me.

(In the gloom at the back **ARTHUR** *appears. He is wearing an opera hat and cape. He is very miserable. He expects and dreads* **LINDA***'s indifference but hopes that some miraculous change of heart may occur any minute.)*

ARTHUR. *(tentatively)* Good evening, Linda.

LINDA. Hello, Arthur. Arthur, I'd like you to meet my aunt, Mrs. Rowena Stoker.

ARTHUR. It's a great pleasure to meet you, Mrs. Stoker. I hope I'm not intruding. I was just passing by and I thought…

(His voice trails off.)

ROWENA. We thought there was going to be a rehearsal of the new pantomime we're engaged for, Mr. Warburton. But nobody's showed up, so like as not we mistook the day. Linda's just been practicing a few steps for practice, haven't you, dovie?

LINDA. *(by rote)* Arthur, we were just going to have a little supper. We hope you'll have some with us. Just a kippered herring and some tea.

ARTHUR. That's awfully good of you. I've just come from dinner. But I hope you won't mind if I sit by you, Mrs. Stoker.

ROWENA. Suit yourself, I always say. It isn't very attractive in an empty theatre. But you must have something, oh yes.

LINDA. Perhaps you'd like to do us a favor, Arthur. Joey's downstairs doing the cooking and can't go. Perhaps you'd like to go down to the corner and bring us a jug of ale and bitters.

ROWENA. I have a shilling here somewhere.

LINDA. Aunt Rowena, perhaps Arthur is dressed too grand to go to a pub...

ROWENA. The pubs in this street is used to us coming in in all kinds of costumes, Mr. Warburton. They'll think you're rehearsing for a society play.

ARTHUR. *(who has refused the shilling, and is all feverish willingness)* I'll be right back. I'll only be a minute, Mrs. Stoker.

(He hurries out.)

ROWENA. The poor boy is off his head for sure. Makes me feel all old just to see him. But I imagine he's quite a nice young man when he's got his senses. But never mind, Linda, nobody wants you to marry anybody you don't want to marry. – Has he been drinking, dearie, or does he just look that way?

LINDA. He just looks that way.

*(Enter **JOEY**, with cups, knives, forks, etc.)*

JOEY. Where's the duke?

ROWENA. He's gone to the corner for some ale and bitters. Thank God, he's eaten already. Now Joey, listen. This young man is off his head about Linda, crazy for sure. Now this is serious. Linda says he talks wild and might even be thinking of shooting her. (**JOEY** *whistles.*) Well, the papers are full of such things, Joey. And plays are full of it. It might be. It might be.

JOEY. Well, I've heard about such things, but it never happened in my family.

ROWENA. Just the same we must take steps. Joey, I'll have him take his cape off. You take it downstairs and see if there's anything in the pocket.

JOEY. What in the pocket?

ROWENA. Why...one of those small guns.

LINDA. Yes, of course, there's one in his pocket. I know there is.

ROWENA. It would be in his cape so as not to bulge his other pockets. Listen, Joey, if there is a gun there, you take out the bullets, and then put the gun back into his pocket empty. See? Then bring the cape back again. If this boy is going to shoot Linda, he's going to shoot her tonight, so we can have a good heart-to-heart talk about it.

JOEY. Yes, and then call the police, that's what!

ROWENA. No, this is a thing police and prisons can't cure. Now, Joey, if you find a gun in his pocket and have done what I told you, you come back on the stage whistling one of your songs. Whistle your song about bank holidays. You know "My holiday girl on a holiday bus."

JOEY. Right-a!

ROWENA. Now, Linda, you act just natural. Let him have his murder and get it out of his system. Yes, you know I like the boy and I don't hold it against him. When we're twenty-one years old we all have a few drops of crazy melodrama in us.

LINDA. (*suddenly*) Oh, I hate him, I 'ate 'im! Why can't he let me be?

ROWENA. Yes, yes. That's love.

LINDA. (*on the verge of hysterics*) Auntie, can't it be cured? Can't you make him just forget me?

ROWENA. Well, dovie, they say there are some ways. Some say you can make fun of him and mock him out of it. And some say you can show yourself up at your worst or pretend you're worse than you are. But I say there's only one way to cure that kind of love when it's fever-ish and all upset.

(*She pauses, groping for her thought.*)

Only love can cure love. Only being interested...only being real interested and fond of him can...can...

(*She gives it up.*)

ROWENA. *(cont.)* It's all right, dearie. Don't you get jumpy. It's a lucky chance to get the thing cleared up. Only remember this: I like him. I like him. He's just some-body's boy that's not well for a few weeks.

LINDA. He breathes too hard.

(Enter ARTHUR, *followed by* JOEY. ARTHUR*'s hands are laden with bundles and bottles.)*

ROWENA. Why, Mr. Warburton, I never see such a load. Whatever did you find to bring? Fries? Salami, and I don't know what all. This is a feast. Take off your coat, Mr. Warburton. Joey, help Mr. Warburton off with his coat. Take it and hang it on the peg downstairs.

ARTHUR. *(with concern)* I think I'll keep the coat, thanks.

ROWENA. *(as* JOEY *attacks it)* Oh, no, no! You won't need your coat. There's nothing worse than sitting about in a heavy coat.

*(*ARTHUR *follows it with his eyes, as* JOEY *bears it off.)*

But Linda, you've been exercising. You slip that scarf about you, dearie, and draw up your chair. Well, this is going to be nice. What's nicer than friends sitting down to a bite to eat? And extra nice for you, Mr. Warburton, because you ought to be in your university, or am I mistaken?

ARTHUR. Yes, I ought to be at Cambridge.

ROWENA. Fancy that! It must be exciting to break the rule so boldly. Ah, well, life is so dull that it does us good every now and then to make a little excitement. Now, Mr. Warburton, you'll change your mind and have a little snack with us. A slice of salami?

ARTHUR. I don't think I could eat anything. I'll have a little ale.

ROWENA. *(busying herself over the table)* That's right.

ARTHUR. *(ventures a word to* LINDA*)* Madame Angellelli is having a soiree Thursday, Linda. Don't you go any more?

LINDA. No, I don't like them.

ARTHUR. I wondered where you were last Thursday. Madame Angellelli expected you every minute.

LINDA. I don't like them.

(silence)

ROWENA. What can be keeping Joey over the kipper? Have you seen Joey on the stage, Mr. Warburton? – Joey Weston he is.

ARTHUR. No, I don't think I have.

ROWENA. Oh, very fine, he is! Quite the best comedian in the pantomimes. But surely you must have seen his wife. She was Henrietta du Vaux. She was the most popular soubrette in all England, and very famous, she was. He lost her two years ago, Henrietta du Vaux. Everybody loved her. It was a terrible loss. Shh-here he comes!

(Enter **JOEY** *with the kipper and the tea. He is jubilantly whistling a tune that presently breaks out into the words: "A holiday girl on a holiday bus.")*

What a noise you do make, Joey, for sure. Anybody'd think you were happy about something. Well, now, Mr. Warburton, you'll excuse us if we sit down and fall right to.

*(***ARTHUR*** sits at the left turned toward them.* **JOEY** *faces the audience, with* **ROWENA** *and* **LINDA** *facing one another,* **ROWENA** *at his right and* **LINDA** *at his left.)*

JOEY. It's cold here, Rowena, after the kitchen.

ROWENA. Yes, it's colder than I thought for. Joey, go and get Mr. Warburton's coat for him. I think he'll want it after all.

ARTHUR. Yes, I'd better keep it by me.

(He follows **JOEY** *to the door and takes the coat from him.)*

ROWENA. *(while the men are at the door)* How do you feel, dearie?

LINDA. I hate it. I wish I were home.

ROWENA. Joey, this is good. You're a good cook.

*(They eat absorbedly for a few moments; then **ROWENA** gazes out into the vault of the dark theatre.)*

Oh, this old theatre has seen some wonderful nights! I'll never forget you, Joey, in Robinson Crusoe the Second. I'll never forget you standing right there and pretending you saw a ghost. I hurt myself laughing.

JOEY. No, it wasn't me. It was Henrietta. She sang *The Sultan of Bagdad* three hundred times in this very house. On these very same boards. Three hundred times the house went crazy when she sang *The Houseboat Song.* They'd sit so quiet you'd think they were holding their breaths, and then they'd break out into shouts and cries. Henrietta du Vaux was my wife, Mr. Warburton. She was the best soubrette in England since Nell Gwynne, sir.

ROWENA. I can hear her now, Joey. She was as good a friend as she was a singer.

JOEY. After the show I would be waiting for her at the corner, Mr. Warburton. *(He points to the corner.)* Do you know the corner, sir?

ARTHUR. *(fascinated)* Yes.

JOEY. I did not always have an engagement and the manager did not think it right to have a husband waiting in the theatre to take the soubrette home. So I waited for her at that corner. She slipped away from all that applause, sir, to go home with a husband that did not always have an engagement.

ROWENA. Joey, I won't have you saying that. You're one of the best comics in England. – Joey, you're tired. Rest yourself a bit.

JOEY. No, Rowena, I want to say this about her. She never felt her success. And she had a hundred ways of pretending that she was no success at all. "Joey," she'd say, "I got it all wrong tonight." And then she'd ask me how she should do it.

ROWENA. Do draw up a chair, Mr. Warburton, and have a bite for good feelings' sake. We're all friends here. Linda, put a piece of sausage on some bread for him, with your own hands.

ARTHUR. Well, thanks, thank you very much.

JOEY. *(with increasing impressiveness)* And when she was ill, she knew that her coughing hurt me. And she'd suffer four times over trying to hold back her coughing. "Cough, Henrietta," I'd say, "if it makes you more comfortable." But no! – she'd act like I was the sick person that had to be taken care of. *(turning on* **ARTHUR** *with gravity and force)* I read in the papers about people who shoot the persons they love. I don't know what to think. What is it but that they want to be noticed, noticed even if they must shoot to get noticed? It's themselves – it's themselves they love.

*(***JOEY*** *stares at* **ARTHUR** *so fixedly that* **ARTHUR** *breathes an all but involuntary "Yes," then rises abruptly and says:)*

ARTHUR. I must go now. You've been very kind.

ROWENA. *(rising)* Joey, come downstairs with me a minute and help me open that old chest. I think we can find Henrietta's shield and spear from *The Palace of Ice* and other things. The lock's been broken for years.

JOEY. All right, Rowena. Let's look.

ROWENA. We won't be a minute. You go on eating.

(They go out.)

ARTHUR. I won't trouble you any more, Linda. I want you to be happy, that's all.

LINDA. You don't trouble me, Arthur.

ARTHUR. What he said is true. I want to be noticed. I wish you liked me, Linda. I mean I wish you liked me more. I wish I could prove to you that I'd do anything for you. That I could bring to you all…that…that he was describing…I won't be a trouble to you any more.

ARTHUR. *(cont.)* *(He turns.)* I can prove it to you, Linda. I've been waiting at that corner for hours, just walking up and down. And I'd planned, Linda, to prove that I couldn't live without you…and if you were going to be cold and…didn't like me, Linda, I was going to shoot myself right here…to prove to you.

(He puts the revolver on the table.)

To prove to you. – But you've all been so kind to me. And that…and Mr. Weston told about his wife. I think just loving isn't wasted.

(He weeps silently.)

LINDA. *(horrified)* Arthur! I wish you wouldn't!

ARTHUR. I imagine I'm…I'm young still. – Good-bye and thanks. Good-bye.

*(He hurries out. **LINDA** shudders with distaste; peers at the revolver; starts to walk about the room and presently is sketching steps again. **JOEY** and **ROWENA** return.)*

ROWENA. Was that he that went out? What happened, Linda?

LINDA. *(interrupting her drill, indifferently)* He said goodbye forever. He left the gun to prove to me something or other. Thank you for nothing.

ROWENA. Linda, I hope you said a nice word to him.

LINDA. Thank you for nothing, I said.

ROWENA. Well, young lady, you're only sixteen. Wait till your turn comes. We'll have to take care of you.

LINDA. Don't let's talk about it. It makes me tired. So hot and excited and breathing so hard. Mario would never act like that. Mario…Mario doesn't even seem to notice you when you're there…

End of Play

SUCH THINGS ONLY HAPPEN
IN BOOKS

CHARACTERS

JOHN, a young novelist
GABRIELLE, his wife
DOCTOR BUMPAS, the local doctor
MR. GRAHAM, John's friend, around fifty

SETTING

An old house in a New Hampshire village.

*(This is **JOHN**'s library and study and living room in one. It is a spring evening. **JOHN** is playing solitaire on a card table before the hearth and **GABRIELLE** is sewing.)*

(silence)

*(**JOHN** finishes a game, takes up his fountain pen, makes a notation on a piece of paper beside him, and starts shuffling the cards.)*

JOHN. Five.

GABRIELLE. What, dear?

JOHN. Five.

GABRIELLE. Oh!...Even that's more than the average.

JOHN. The average is two. Listen to the scores this evening: zero, two, five, three, zero, one, four, zero, three, one six, zero, zero, zero, three, zero, six, and now five. The full fifty-two come out every twenty-one times. So that from now on my chances for getting it out increase seven point three two every game.

GABRIELLE. *(not understanding, but thinking that this is an unfortunate announcement)* Tchk-Tchk!

(pause)

JOHN. The doctor's still upstairs, isn't he?

GABRIELLE. Yes.

JOHN. It does seem that he's taking an awfully long time.

GABRIELLE. Yes, every other day he changes the dressing on the wounds, or burns, or whatever you call it. It takes about half an hour. I offered to help him but he didn't seem to need me. He'll call down the stairs if he needs us.

JOHN. Well, he certainly is taking a long time. Does it hurt Katie when the dressing is changed?

GABRIELLE. Not any more. *(pause)* When's this man coming?

JOHN. About half past eight, I imagine. He may not come at all. He had to work tonight on some sort of report. I just told him to drop around if he'd like and we'd have a game of chess.

GABRIELLE. On his first call like that, I really ought to have thought about getting together something special for him to eat.

JOHN. No, no. I told him you and I always had some cocoa about half past ten – cocoa and biscuits, I said.

GABRIELLE. Well, it's too bad Katie's laid up. I wonder he didn't hear about Katie. The whole town seems to know about her pouring all that boiling water over her legs.

JOHN. Here's another zero, I'm afraid – though it promised very well.

GABRIELLE. How'd you meet this man?

JOHN. Where I meet everybody. At the post office Sunday morning waiting for the mail. People stop in on the way home from church and everybody falls into conversation with everybody else.

GABRIELLE. That's the way you met Miss Buckingham. The unexplained Miss Buckingham. The Miss Buckingham whom I soundly disliked. Why on earth she wanted to poke into this house is still a mystery to me.

JOHN. Anyway she's left town for good now. She's gone back to Australia. – On the whole, though, dear, you don't mind my bringing home stray acquaintances from time to time, do you?

GABRIELLE. Oh, no indeed! Usually I like it.

JOHN. We authors should make it our business to multiply just such acquaintances.

GABRIELLE. By all means. I like it.

JOHN. Besides, this Mr..... Mr.....

GABRIELLE. Graham.

JOHN. Yes, this Mr. Graham asked to come. He said he'd often admired the house sitting up among its elms. I told him it was over two hundred years old and that it had a story. These westerners take a great fancy to our New Hampshire local color. – Really, Gabrielle, the doctor's taking an awfully long time upstairs.

GABRIELLE. Did you tell Mr. Graham the story about the house?

JOHN. No. Anyway I don't really know it. Two young people frightened their father to death – killed him or frightened him to death. I must ask one of the old citizens about it. Every old house in the state claims its murder. Thank God I have too much literary conscience to write another novel about an old New England house.

GABRIELLE. Just the same, let's ask the doctor to tell us all about it. He'll know.

JOHN. *(examining his game)* Well, I guess this is stuck. It really looked as though it were coming out. I can see that if I moved just one card it would open up a lot of combinations.

GABRIELLE. *(without malice)* But you have too much conscience.

JOHN. Yes. – You see it's like fiction. You have to adjust the cards to make a plot. In life most people live along without plots. A plot breaks through about once in every twenty-one times.

GABRIELLE. Well, then, I think a plot is just about due.

JOHN. Not unless we push back the cards and look under. – At all events, this one's no good. I'll take my pipe out into the garden and walk about.

GABRIELLE. Well, keep one eye on the gate, will you? I don't want to open the door to this Mr. Graham without being introduced.

JOHN. All right. I'll walk up and down in front of the house so I won't miss him. I'll leave the front door open; you might whistle to me when the doctor comes downstairs. *(He leans over the tobacco jar, filling his pipe.)* Plots. Plots. If I had no conscience I could choose anyone of these plots that are in everybody's novels and in nobody's lives. These poor battered old plots. Enoch Arden returns and looks through the window and sees his wife married to another.

GABRIELLE. I've always loved that one.

JOHN. The plot that murderers always steal back to the scene of their crime and gloat over the place.

GABRIELLE. Oh, John! How wonderful. They'll come back to this house. Imagine!

JOHN. The plot that all married women of thirty-five have lovers.

GABRIELLE. Otherwise known as the Marseillaise.

JOHN. They're as pathetic and futile as the type-jokes you know that mothers-in-law are unpleasant, that…that cooks feed chicken and turkey to policemen and other callers in the kitchen…

GABRIELLE. Katie! Katie! – Once every twenty-one times these plots really do happen in real life, you say?

JOHN. Once in a thousand. Books and plays are a quiet, harmless fraud about life…

GABRIELLE. Well, now, don't get excited, dear, or you won't be able to work.

JOHN. All right. One pipeful.

(He goes out into the garden. The debonair young **DOCTOR** *comes in from the right. Hat and coat and satchel. He looks inquiringly at* **GABRIELLE***. She makes a sign to him that* **JOHN** *is before the house. She looks out of the door, is reassured, and smiles. The* **DOCTOR** *takes her in his arms. They kiss with conjugal tranquility.)*

GABRIELLE. Ouch!

DR. BUMPAS. Ouch! Ouch!

GABRIELLE. How's Katie?

DR. BUMPAS. Katie, ma'am, will get better. I've got to run along.

GABRIELLE. Oh, stay a minute!

DR. BUMPAS. Very busy. Patients dying like flies.

GABRIELLE. Tchk-Tchk!

DR. BUMPAS. You wouldn't detain me, would you, on my errands of mercy? Hundreds, ma'am, are waiting for my step on the stair.

(He puts down his coat and hat and satchel and kisses her again.)

Twins are popping all over the place – every now and then an appendix goes tttttt – bang. Where'd you get that dress? Very chic, very eye-filling. – Can I trust you with a secret, Gabrielle? Would you like to know a secret?

GABRIELLE. Yes, but hurry. – Don't coquette about it. I told John I'd whistle to him when you came downstairs.

DR. BUMPAS. It's about Katie.

GABRIELLE. Goodness. Katie has no secrets.

DR. BUMPAS. And promise me it won't make any difference between you and Katie. Katie's a fine girl. If you were a stuffy old woman you'd probably fetch up a lot of indignation. And promise not to tell your husband.

GABRIELLE. Oh, I never tell John anything! It would prevent his working.

DR. BUMPAS. Katie just confessed to me how the accident happened. *(a short laugh)* Weren't you surprised that a strong careful girl like Katie could spill a kettle of boiling water over her legs?

GABRIELLE. I certainly was. I thought it very funny indeed.

DR. BUMPAS. Well, it was her brother that did it.

GABRIELLE. I didn't know she had a brother.

DR. BUMPAS. He's been in prison for eight years with four
to go. Forgeries and embezzlements and things. But
not a bad fellow, you know. Used to be an orderly in
my hospital in Boston. Well, three months ago he
escaped from prison. Sirens at midnight *(He winds
the alarm.)*, bloodhounds *(He barks.)*, but he escaped.
Gabrielle, did you ever use to hear noises in your
kitchen at night?

GABRIELLE. I certainly did. I certainly did. But, then, this
house is full of noises. I'd just turn over in bed and say:
Not until that ghost comes into this room will I do anything about it.

DR. BUMPAS. Well, it wasn't a ghost. It was Katie's brother.
Katie's brother has been hidden, living in your house
for three months.

GABRIELLE. Without our knowing it! Why Katie's a mon-
ster.

DR. BUMPAS. Oh, Katie's in anguish about it. What Katie
suffered from burns was nothing compared to what
Katie suffered from conscience. Katie is as honest as
the day. Every single time that Katie fed her brother a
dinner out of your kitchen she went without a dinner
herself. And the rest of his meals she paid for out of
her own pocket money.

GABRIELLE. My, isn't life complicated!

DR. BUMPAS. That night she had boiled some water to wash
the brother's shirts and socks. He lifted the kettle
off the stove and, not being used to hot handles, he
dropped it and the water fell all over Katie's knees. I
can tell you all this now because he has safely crossed
over into Canada to get some work. And now I too
must go.

GABRIELLE. You must see John a minute. *(She whistles.)* It's a
lovely evening. The rain has stopped. John's expecting
a visitor tonight, to play chess. Do you know a west-
erner named Graham?

*(Enter **JOHN.**)*

JOHN. Hello, doctor, you've been a long time about it. How's Katie?

DR. BUMPAS. Katie'll get well. She'll be up and about in a few days.

*(The **DOCTOR** takes up his things.)*

JOHN. Can't you stay a while? Gabrielle'll make us some cocoa.

DR. BUMPAS. Cocoa! Are people still drinking cocoa? – No, I've got to hurry on. Patients dying like flies. Must look in at the hospital again.

GABRIELLE. Oh, I know! Every time he enters the door of the hospital, the building almost leaves the ground.

DR. BUMPAS. I galvanize'm. I galvanize'm. – How's your new book getting on?

JOHN. Nothing begun yet. Groping about for a plot.

DR. BUMPAS. Life's full of plots.

JOHN. We like to think so. But when you come down to it, the rank and file – rich and poor – live much as we do. Not much plot. Work and a nice wife and a nice house and a nice Katie.

DR. BUMPAS. No, no, no – life's full of plots. Swarming with 'em.

JOHN. Here's Mr. Graham now.

*(**JOHN** goes to the door and shakes hands with a reticent bearded man of about fifty. Presentations.)*

MR. GRAHAM. I just stopped by to meet your wife and to explain that I'll have to come another time, if you'll be so good as to ask me.

GABRIELLE. Oh, I'm sorry.

MR. GRAHAM. Tonight I must work. I've been ordered to send in a report and I shall probably work all night. *(looking about)* It's a very interesting, a very attractive house.

JOHN. And it has a story. I was just going to ask Dr. Bumpas to tell it to us.

DR. BUMPAS. Let's see…what was their name?

GABRIELLE. They call it the Hamburton place.

DR. BUMPAS. That's it. It must have been some thirty years ago. There was an old father, rich, hateful, miserly, beard and everything. And he buried a lot of money under the floor or between the bricks.

(He points to the hearth.) There was a son and daughter he kept in rags. Yes, sir, rags, and they lived on potato peelings. They wanted just enough money to get some education and something to wear. And one night they meant to frighten him – they tied him with rope or something to frighten him into releasing some money. Some say they meant to kill him; anyway he died in this very room.

GABRIELLE. What became of the children?

DR. BUMPAS. They disappeared. Tell the truth, no one tried very hard to find them.

GABRIELLE. Did they get any money?

DR. BUMPAS. We hope so. Let's hope they found some. Most of it lies down there in the bank to this day.

JOHN. Well, there you have it.

MR. GRAHAM. Very interesting.

GABRIELLE. Come now, can't you both stay and have a cup of cocoa? It won't take a minute.

DR. BUMPAS. Patients dying like flies. Very glad to have met you, Mr. Graham. – Zzzzt. Off I go.

(He goes out.)

JOHN. All these houses collect folklore like moss.

(to **GABRIELLE***)* You see there's nothing one can make out of a story like that – it's too naïf.

GABRIELLE. Excuse me, one minute. I hear Katie's cowbell. We have a maid upstairs sick in bed, Mr. Graham. When she needs me she rings a cowbell.

(She goes out right.)

MR. GRAHAM. But I must go too. You'll say good night for me. – One question before I go. Did you know a Miss Buckingham, by any chance?

JOHN. Yes, oh, yes. Miss Buckingham came and spent an evening with us here. Yes, she used to be a trained nurse in South Africa, or Australia. She went back there. Did you know her?

MR. GRAHAM. Yes, I used to know her.

JOHN. She liked this house too. She asked to come and see it.

MR. GRAHAM. And she went back to Australia? That's what I wanted to know.

(**GABRIELLE**'s *voice calls,* "*John! John!*")

JOHN. There's my wife calling me upstairs. – You probably can get Miss Buckingham's address at Mrs. Thorpe's boardinghouse. She stayed there. – I'm coming! You'll excuse me. Just come any time, Mr. Graham, and we'll have a game.

(**JOHN** *hurries out.* **MR. GRAHAM**, *who has been at the front door, reenters, crosses the room with grave caution to the front right corner. He slowly picks up one corner of the carpet and stares at a mottled portion of the floor. He lowers the carpet and goes out into the street.* **JOHN** *and* **GABRIELLE** *return.*)

JOHN. I guess she'll be comfortable now.

GABRIELLE. Here you see here's our evening free after all.

JOHN. Didn't even have the excitement of a game of chess. Well, I like it best this way.

(*He sits down to his cards again.* **GABRIELLE** *takes up her sewing, then rises and stands behind him watching the game over his shoulder.*)

GABRIELLE. There! That jack on the ten releases the ace.

JOHN. But even then we're at a standstill.

GABRIELLE. I don't see why that game shouldn't come out oftener.

(pause)

I don't think you see all the moves.

JOHN. I certainly do see all the moves that are to be seen. – You don't expect me to look under the cards, do you?

(He sweeps the cards toward him and starts to shuffle.)

One more game and then we'll have some cocoa.

End of Play

THE HAPPY JOURNEY TO TRENTON AND CAMDEN

CHARACTERS

THE STAGE MANAGER

MA, Mrs. Kate Kirby

ARTHUR, thirteen, her son

CAROLINE, fifteen, her daughter

PA

BEULAH, twenty-two, the Kirbys' married daughter who lives in Camden, New Jersey

SETTING

The Kirby house; then the Kirby family car trip from Newark to Camden, New Jersey.

NOTES TO THE PRODUCER

Although the speech, manner and business of the actors is colloquial and realistic, the production should stimulate the imagination and be implied and suggestive. All properties, except two, are imaginary, but their use is to be carried with detailed pantomime. One of these two is the automobile, which is made up of four chairs on a low platform. In some productions, because of the sight lines of the auditorium, it has been found necessary to raise slightly the two rear chairs of the automobile. The second is an ordinary cot or couch.

The Stage Manager not only moves forward and withdraws these two properties, but he reads from a typescript the lines of all the minor (invisible) characters. He reads them clearly, but with little attempt at characterization, even when he responds in the person of a child or a woman. He may smoke, read a newspaper and eat an apple throughout the course of the play. He should never be obtrusive nor distract the attention of the audience from the central action.

It should constantly be borne in mind that the purpose of this play is the portrayal of the character of Ma Kirby, the author at one time having even considered entitling the play "The Portrait of a Lady." Accordingly, the director should constantly keep in mind that Ma Kirby's humor, strength and humanity constitute the unifying element throughout. This aspect should always rise above the merely humorous characteristic details of the play.

Many productions have fallen into two regrettable extremes. On the one hand actors have exaggerated the humorous characters and situations in the direction of farce; and on the other hand, have treated Ma Kirby's sentiment and religion with sentimentality and preachy solemnity. The atmosphere, comedy, and characterization of this play are most effective when they are handled with great simplicity and evenness.

Thornton Wilder, 1931

(No scenery is required for this play. The idea is that no place is being represented. This may be achieved by a gray curtain back-drop with no side-pieces; a cyclorama; or the empty bare stage.)

(As the curtain rises **THE STAGE MANAGER** *is leaning lazily against the proscenium pillar at the audiences left. He is smoking.)*

*(***ARTHUR*** is playing marbles in the center of the stage in pantomime.)*

*(***CAROLINE*** is at the remote back right talking to some girls who are invisible to us.)*

*(***MA KIRBY*** is anxiously putting on her hat [real] before an imaginary mirror.)*

MA. Where's your pa? Why isn't he here? I declare we'll never get started.

ARTHUR. Ma, where's my hat? I guess I don't go if I can't find my hat. *(still playing marbles)*

MA. Go out into the hall and see if it isn't there. Where's Caroline gone to now, the plagued child?

ARTHUR. She's out waitin' in the street talkin' to the Jones girls. – I just looked in the hall a thousand times, Ma, and it isn't there. *(He spits for good luck before a difficult shot and mutters:)* Come on, baby.

MA. Go and look again, I say. Look carefully.

*(***ARTHUR*** rises, runs to the right, turns around swiftly, returns to his game, flinging himself on the floor with a terrible impact and starts shooting an aggie.)*

ARTHUR. No, Ma, it's not there.

MA. *(serenely)* Well, you don't leave Newark without that hat, make up your mind to that. I don't go no journeys with a hoodlum.

ARTHUR. Aw, Ma!

(**MA** *comes down to the footlights and talks toward the audience as through a window.*)

MA. *(calling)* Oh, Mrs. Schwartz!

THE STAGE MANAGER. *(consulting his script)* Here I am, Mrs. Kirby. Are you going yet?

MA. I guess we're going in just a minute. How's the baby?

THE STAGE MANAGER. She's all right now. We slapped her on the back and she spat it up.

MA. Isn't that fine! – Well now, if you'll be good enough to give the cat a saucer of milk in the morning and the evening, Mrs. Schwartz, I'll be ever so grateful to you. – Oh, good afternoon, Mrs. Hobmeyer!

THE STAGE MANAGER. Good afternoon, Mrs. Kirby, I hear you're going away.

MA. *(modest)* Oh, just for three days, Mrs. Hobmeyer, to see my married daughter, Beulah, in Camden. Elmer's got his vacation week from the laundry early this year, and he's just the best driver in the world.

(**CAROLINE** *comes "into the house" and stands by her mother.*)

THE STAGE MANAGER. Is the whole family going?

MA. Yes, all four of us that's here. The change ought to be good for the children. My married daughter was downright sick a while ago –

THE STAGE MANAGER. Tchk-Tchk-Tchk! Yes. I remember you tellin' us.

MA. And I just want to go down and see the child. I ain't seen her since then. I just won't rest easy in my mind without I see her. *(to* **CAROLINE***)* Can't you say good afternoon to Mrs. Hobmeyer?

CAROLINE. *(blushes and lowers her eyes and says woodenly)* Good afternoon, Mrs. Hobmeyer.

THE STAGE MANAGER. Good afternoon, dear. – Well, I'll wait and beat these rugs after you're gone, because I don't want to choke you. I hope you have a good time and find everything all right.

MA. Thank you, Mrs. Hobmeyer, I hope I will. – Well, I guess that milk for the cat is all, Mrs. Schwartz, if you're sure you don't mind. If anything should come up, the key to the back door is hanging by the icebox.

CAROLINE. Ma! Not so loud.

ARTHUR. Everybody can hear yuh.

MA. Stop pullin' my dress, children. *(in a loud whisper)* The key to the back door I'll leave hangin' by the icebox and I'll leave the screen door unhooked.

THE STAGE MANAGER. Now have a good trip, dear, and give my love to Loolie.

MA. I will, and thank you a thousand times.

(She lowers the window, turns up stage and looks around. **CAROLINE** *goes left and vigorously rubs her cheeks.* **MA** *occupies herself with the last touches of packing.)*

What can be keeping your pa?

ARTHUR. *(who has not left his marbles)* I can't find my hat, Ma.

(Enter **ELMER** *holding a hat.)*

ELMER. Here's Arthur's hat. He musta left it in the car Sunday.

MA. That's a mercy. Now we can start. – Caroline Kirby, what you done to your cheeks?

CAROLINE. *(defiant, abashed)* Nothin'.

MA. If you've put anything on 'em, I'll slap you.

CAROLINE. No, Ma, of course I haven't. *(hanging her head)* I just rubbed 'em to make 'em red. All the girls do that at high school when they're goin' places.

MA. Such silliness I never saw. Elmer, what kep' you?

ELMER. *(always even-voiced and always looking out a little anxiously through his spectacles)* I just went to the garage and had Charlie give a last look at it, Kate.

MA. I'm glad you did. *(collecting two pieces of imaginary luggage and starting for the door)* I wouldn't like to have no breakdown miles from anywhere. Now we can start. Arthur, put those marbles away. Anybody'd think you didn't want to go on a journey to look at yuh.

(They go out through the "hall," take the short steps that denote going downstairs, and find themselves in the street.)

ELMER. Here, you boys, you keep away from that car.

MA. Those Sullivan boys put their heads into everything.

*(****THE STAGE MANAGER**** has moved forward four chairs and a low platform. This is the automobile. It is in the center of the stage and faces the audience. The platform slightly raises the two chairs in the rear.* **PA**'s *hands hold an imaginary steering wheel and continually shift gears.* **CAROLINE** *sits beside him.* **ARTHUR** *is behind him and* **MA** *behind* **CAROLINE***)*

CAROLINE. *(self-consciously)* Good-bye, Mildred. Good-bye, Helen.

THE STAGE MANAGER. Good-bye, Caroline. Good-bye, Mrs. Kirby. I hope y'have a good time.

MA. Good-bye, girls.

THE STAGE MANAGER. Good-bye, Kate. The car looks fine.

MA. *(looking upward toward a window)* Oh, good-bye, Emma! *(modestly)* We think it's the best little Chevrolet in the world. – Oh, good-bye, Mrs. Adler!

THE STAGE MANAGER. What, are you going away, Mrs. Kirby?

MA. Just for three days, Mrs. Adler, to see my married daughter in Camden.

THE STAGE MANAGER. Have a good time.

(Now **MA, CAROLINE** *and* **THE STAGE MANAGER** *break out into a tremendous chorus of good-byes. The whole street is saying good-bye.* **ARTHUR** *takes out his pea-shooter and lets fly happily into the air. There is a lurch or two and they are off.)*

ARTHUR. *(in sudden fright)* Pa! Pa! Don't go by the school. Mr. Biedenbach might see us!

MA. I don't care if he does see us. I guess I can take my children out of school for one day without having to hide down back streets about it.

(ELMER nods to a passerby. MA asks without sharpness.)

Who was that you spoke to, Elmer?

ELMER. That was the fellow who arranges our banquets down to the lodge, Kate.

MA. Is he the one who had to buy four hundred steaks? *(PA nods.)* I declare, I'm glad I'm not him.

ELMER. The air's getting better already. Take deep breaths, children.

(They inhale noisily.)

ARTHUR. *(pointing to a sign and indicating that it gradually goes by)* Gee, it's almost open fields already. *"Weber and Heilbronner Suits for Well-Dressed Men."* Ma, can I have one of them some day?

MA. If you graduate with good marks perhaps your father'll let you have one for graduation.

(Pause. General gazing about and then a sudden lurch.)

CAROLINE. *(whining)* Oh, Pa! Do we have to wait while that whole funeral goes by?

(PA takes off his hat. MA cranes forward with absorbed curiosity.)

MA. Take off your hat, Arthur. Look at your father. – Why, Elmer, I do believe that's a lodge brother of yours. See the banner? I suppose this is the Elizabeth branch.

(ELMER nods. MA sighs Tchk-tchk-tchk. They all lean forward and watch the funeral in silence, growing momentarily more solemnized. After a pause, MA continues almost dreamily but not sentimentaly:)

Well, we haven't forgotten the funeral that we went on, have we? We haven't forgotten our good Harold. He gave his life for his country, we mustn't forget that.

(She passes her finger from the corner of her eye across her cheek. There is another pause, with cheerful resignation.)

MA. *(cont.)* Well, we'll all hold up the traffic for a few minutes some day.

THE CHILDREN. *(very uncomfortable)* Ma!

MA. *(without self-pity)* Well I'm "ready," children. I hope everybody in this car is "ready."

(She puts her hand on PA's shoulder.)

And I pray to go first, Elmer. Yes.

(PA touches her hand.)

CAROLINE. Ma, everybody's looking at you.

ARTHUR. Everybody's laughing at you.

MA. Oh, hold your tongues! I don't care what a lot of silly people in Elizabeth, New Jersey, think of me. – Now we can go on. That's the last.

(There is another lurch and the car goes on.)

CAROLINE. *(looking at a sign and turning as she passes it)* "Fit-Rite Suspenders. The Working Man's Choice." Pa, why do they spell Rite that way?

ELMER. So that it'll make you stop and ask about it, Missy.

CAROLINE. Papa, you're teasing me. – Ma, why do they say "*Three Hundred Rooms Three Hundred Baths?*"

ARTHUR. "*Millers Spaghetti: The Family's Favorite Dish.*" Ma, why don't you ever have spaghetti?

MA. Go along, you'd never eat it.

ARTHUR. Ma, I like it now.

CAROLINE. *(with gesture)* Yum-yum. It looks wonderful up there. Ma, make some when we get home?

MA. *(dryly)* "The management is always happy to receive suggestions. We aim to please."

(The whole family finds this exquisitely funny. The children scream with laughter. Even **ELMER** *smiles.* **MA** *remains modest)*

ELMER. Well, I guess no one's complaining, Kate. Everybody knows you're a good cook.

MA. I don't know whether I'm a good cook or not, but I know I've had practice. At least I've cooked three meals a day for twenty-five years.

ARTHUR. Aw, Ma, you went out to eat once in a while.

MA. Yes. That made it a leap year.

(This joke is no less successful than its predecessor. When the laughter dies down, **CAROLINE** *turns around in an ecstasy of well-being, and kneeling on the cushions says.)*

CAROLINE. Ma, I love going out in the country like this. Let's do it often, Ma.

MA. Goodness, smell that air will you! It's got the whole ocean in it. – Elmer, drive careful over that bridge. This must be New Brunswick we're coming to.

ARTHUR. *(jealous of his mother's successes)* Ma, when is the next comfort station?

MA. *(unruffled)* You don't want one. You just said that to be awful.

CAROLINE. *(shrilly)* Yes, he did, Ma. He's terrible. He says that kind of thing right out in school and I want to sink through the floor, Ma. He's terrible.

MA. Oh, don't get so excited about nothing, Miss Proper! I guess we're all yewman-beings in this car, at least as far as I know. And, Arthur, you try and be a gentleman. – Elmer, don't run over that collie dog.

(She follows the dog with her eyes.)

Looked kinda peaked to me. Needs a good honest bowl of leavings. Pretty dog, too.

(Her eyes fall on a billboard.)

That's a pretty advertisement for Chesterfield cigarettes, isn't it? Looks like Beulah, a little.

ARTHUR. Ma?

MA. Yes.

ARTHUR. Can't I take a paper route *("route" rhymes with "out")* with the *Newark Daily Post?*

MA. No, you cannot. No, sir. I hear they make the paper-boys get up at four-thirty in the morning. No son of mine is going to get up at four-thirty every morning, not if it's to make a million dollars. Your *Saturday Evening Post* route on Thursday mornings is enough.

ARTHUR. Aw, Ma.

MA. No, sir. No son of mine is going to get up at four-thirty and miss the sleep God meant him to have.

ARTHUR. *(sullenly)* Hhm! Ma's always talking about God. I guess she got a letter from him this morning.

(MA rises, outraged.)

MA. Elmer, stop that automobile this minute. I don't go another step with anybody that says things like that. Arthur, you get out of this car. *(PA stops the car.)* Elmer, you give him a dollar bill. He can go back to Newark, by himself. I don't want him.

ARTHUR. What did I say? There wasn't anything terrible about that.

ELMER. I didn't hear what he said, Kate.

MA. God has done a lot of things for me and I won't have Him made fun of by anybody. Get out of the car this minute.

CAROLINE. Aw, Ma – don't spoil the ride.

MA. No.

ELMER. We might as well go on, Kate, since we've got started. I'll talk to the boy tonight.

MA. *(slowly conceding)* All right, if you say so, Elmer. *(PA starts the car.)* But I won't sit beside him. Caroline, you come, and sit by me.

ARTHUR. *(frightened)* Aw, Ma, that wasn't so terrible.

MA. I don't want to talk about it. I hope your father washes your mouth out with soap and water. – Where'd we all be if I started talking about God like that, I'd like to know! We'd be in the speakeasies and nightclubs and places like that, that's where we'd be. – All right, Elmer, you can go on now.

CAROLINE. *(after a slight pause)* What did he say, Ma? I didn't hear what he said.

MA. I don't want to talk about it.

(They drive on in silence for a moment, the shocked silence after a scandal.)

ELMER. I'm going to stop and give the car a little water, I guess.

MA. All right, Elmer. You know best.

ELMER. *(turns the wheel and stops; to a garage hand:)* Could I have a little water in the radiator – to make sure?

THE STAGE MANAGER. *(In this scene alone he lays aside his script and enters into a role seriously.)* You sure can. *(He punches the tires.)* Air, all right? Do you need any oil or gas?

ELMER. No, I think not. I just got fixed up in Newark.

MA. We're on the right road for Camden, are we?

THE STAGE MANAGER. Yes, keep straight ahead. You can't miss it. You'll be in Trenton in a few minutes.

(He carefully pours some water into the hood.)

Camden's a great town, lady, believe me.

MA. My daughter likes it fine – my married daughter.

THE STAGE MANAGER. Yea? It's a great burg all right. I guess I think so because I was born near there.

MA. Well, well. Your folks still live there?

THE STAGE MANAGER. *(Standing with one foot on the rung of* MA*'s chair. They have taken a great fancy to one another.)* No, my old man sold the farm and they built a factory on it. So the folks moved to Philadelphia.

MA. My married daughter Beulah lives there because her husband works in the telephone company. – Stop pokin' me, Caroline! – We're all going down to see her for a few days.

THE STAGE MANAGER. Yea?

MA. She's been sick, you see, and I just felt I had to go and see her. My husband and my boy are going to stay at the Y.M.C.A. I hear they've got a dormitory on the top floor that's real clean and comfortable. Had you ever been there?

THE STAGE MANAGER. No. I'm Knights of Columbus myself.

MA. Oh.

THE STAGE MANAGER. I used to play basketball at the Y though. It looked all right to me.

(He reluctantly shakes himself out of it and pretends to examine the car again, whistling.)

Well, I guess you're all set now, lady. I hope you have a good trip; you can't miss it.

EVERYBODY. Thanks. Thanks a lot. Good luck to you.

(The car jolts and lurches.)

MA. *(with a sigh)* The world's full of nice people. – That's what I call a nice young man.

CAROLINE. *(earnestly)* Ma, you oughtn't to tell 'em all everything about yourself.

MA. Well, Caroline, you do your way and I'll do mine. – He looked kinda pale to me. I'd like to feed him up for a few days. His mother lives in Philadelphia and I expect he eats at those dreadful Greek places.

CAROLINE. I'm hungry. Pa, there's a hot dog stand. K'n I have one?

ELMER. We'll all have one, eh, Kate? We had such an early lunch.

MA. Just as you think best, Elmer.

(He stops the car.)

ELMER. Arthur, here's half a dollar. Run over and see what they have. Not too much mustard either.

*(**ARTHUR** descends from the car and goes offstage right. **MA** and **CAROLINE** get out and walk a bit.)*

MA. What's that flower over there? I'll take some of those to Beulah.

CAROLINE. It's just a weed, Ma.

MA. I like it. – My, look at the sky, wouldya! I'm glad I was born in New Jersey. I've always said it was the best state in the Union. Every state has something no other state has got.

(They stroll about humming. Presently ARTHUR returns with his hands full of imaginary hot dogs which he distributes. He is still very much cast down by the recent scandal. He finally approaches his mother and says falteringly:)

ARTHUR. Ma, I'm sorry. I'm sorry for what I said.

(He bursts into tears and puts his forehead against her elbow.)

MA. There. There. We all say wicked things at times. I know you didn't mean it like it sounded.

(He weeps still more violently than before.)

Why, now, now! I forgive you, Arthur, and tonight before you go to bed you... *(She whispers.)* You're a good boy at heart, Arthur, and we all know it.

*(**CAROLINE** starts to cry too. **MA** is suddenly joyously alive and happy.)*

Sakes alive, it's too nice a day for us all to be cryin'. Come now, get in. Caroline, go up in front with your father. Ma wants to sit with her beau.

*(**CAROLINE** sits in front with her father. **MA** lets **ARTHUR** get in car ahead of her; then she closes door.)*

I never saw such children. Your hot dogs are all getting wet. Now chew them fine, everybody. – All right, Elmer, forward march.

*(Car starts. **CAROLINE** spits.)*

– Caroline, whatever are you doing?

CAROLINE. I'm spitting out the leather, Ma.

MA. Then say Excuse me.

CAROLINE. Excuse me, please. *(She spits again.)*

MA. What's this place? Arthur, did you see the post office?

ARTHUR. It said Lawrenceville.

MA. Hnn. School kinda. Nice. I wonder what that big yellow house set back was. – Now it's beginning to be Trenton.

CAROLINE. Papa, it was near here that George Washington crossed the Delaware. It was near Trenton, Mama. He was first in war and first in peace and first in the hearts of his countrymen.

MA. (*surveying the passing world, serene and didactic*) Well, the thing I like about him best was that he never told a lie.

(*The children are duly cast down. There is a pause.*)

There's a sunset for you. There's nothing like a good sunset.

ARTHUR. There's an Ohio license in front of us. Ma, have you ever been to Ohio?

MA. No.

(*A dreamy silence descends upon them.* **CAROLINE** *sits closer to her father.* **MA** *puts her arm around* **ARTHUR**, *unsentimentally.*)

ARTHUR. Ma, what a lotta people there are in the world, Ma. There must be thousands and thousands in the United States. Ma, how many are there?

MA. I don't know. Ask your father.

ARTHUR. Pa, how many are there?

ELMER. There are a hundred and twenty-six million, Kate.

MA. (*giving a pressure about* **ARTHUR**'s *shoulder*) And they all like to drive out in the evening with their children beside 'em.

(*another pause*)

Why doesn't somebody sing something? Arthur, you're always singing something; what's the matter with you?

ARTHUR. All right. What'll we sing? (*He sketches:*)

In the Blue Ridge mountains of Virginia,

On the trail of the lonesome pine...

No, I don't like that anymore. Let's do:

I been workin' on de railroad

(**CAROLINE** *joins in.*)

All de liblong day.

(**MA** *sings.*)

I been workin' on de railroad

(**PA** *joins in.*)

Just to pass de time away.

(**MA** *suddenly jumps up with a wild cry.*)

MA. Elmer, that signpost said Camden, I saw it.

ELMER. All right, Kate, if you're sure.

(*much shifting of gears, backing, and jolting*)

MA. Yes, there it is. Camden – five miles. Dear old Beulah. (*The journey continues.*) – Now, children, you be good and quiet during dinner. She's just got out of bed after a big sorta operation, and we must all move around kinda quiet. First you drop me and Caroline at the door and just say hello, and then you menfolk go over to the Y.M.C.A. and come back for dinner in about an hour.

CAROLINE. (*shutting her eyes and pressing her fists passionately against her nose*) I see the first star. Everybody make a wish.

Star light, star bright,

First star I seen tonight.

I wish I may, I wish I might

Have the wish I wish tonight.

(*then solemnly*) Pins. Mama, you say "needles."

(*She interlocks little fingers with her mother.*)

MA. Needles.

CAROLINE. Shakespeare. Ma, you say "Longfellow."

MA. Longfellow.

CAROLINE. Now it's a secret and I can't tell it to anybody. Ma, you make a wish.

MA. *(with almost grim humor)* No, I can make wishes without waiting for no star. And I can tell my wishes right out loud too. Do you want to hear them?

CAROLINE. *(resignedly)* No, Ma, we know 'em already. We've heard 'em.

(She hangs her head affectedly on her mother's left shoulder and says with unmalicious mimicry.)

You want me to be a good girl and you want Arthur to be honest in word and deed.

MA. *(majestically)* Yes. So mind yourself.

ELMER. Caroline, take out that letter from Beulah in my coat pocket by you and read aloud the places I marked with red pencil.

CAROLINE. *(working)* "A few blocks after you pass the two big oil tanks on your left…"

EVERYBODY. *(pointing backward)* There they are!

CAROLINE. "…you come to a corner where there's an A & P store on the left and a firehouse kitty-corner to it…"

(They all jubilantly identify these landmarks.)

"…turn right, go two blocks, and our house is Weyerhauser Street Number 471."

MA. It's an even nicer street than they used to live in. And right handy to an A & P.

CAROLINE. *(whispering)* Ma, it's better than our street. It's richer than our street. – Ma, isn't Beulah richer than we are?

MA. *(looking at her with a firm and glassy eye)* Mind yourself, missy. I don't want to hear anybody talking about rich or not rich when I'm around. If people aren't nice I don't care how rich they are. I live in the best street in the world because my husband and children live there.

*(She glares impressively at **CAROLINE** a moment to let this lesson sink in, then looks up, sees **BEULAH** and waves.)*

There's Beulah standing on the steps lookin' for us.

(**BEULAH** *has appeared and is waving. They all call out "Hello, Beulah – Hello." Presently they are all getting out of the car.*)

BEULAH. Hello, Mama. – Well, lookit how Arthur and Caroline are growing!

MA. They're bursting all their clothes!

BEULAH. (*kisses her father long and affectionately*) Hello, Papa. Good old Papa. You look tired, Pa –

MA. – Yes, your pa needs a rest. Thank Heaven, his vacation has come just now. We'll feed him up and let him sleep late. Pa has a present for you, Loolie. He would go and buy it.

BEULAH. Why, Pa, you're terrible to go and buy anything for me. Isn't he terrible?

MA. Well, it's a secret. You can open it at dinner.

BEULAH. (*puts her arm around his neck and rubs her nose against his temple*) Crazy old Pa, goin' buyin' things! It's me that ought to be buyin' things for you, Pa.

ELMER. Oh, no! There's only one Loolie in the world.

BEULAH. (*whispering, as her eyes fill with tears*) Are you glad I'm still alive, Pa?

(*She kisses him abruptly and goes back to the house steps.*)

ELMER. Where's Horace, Loolie?

BEULAH. He was kep' over a little at the office. He'll be here any minute. He's crazy to see you all.

MA. All right. You men go over to the Y and come back in about an hour.

BEULAH. (*As her father returns to the wheel, she stands out in the street beside him.*) Go straight along, Pa, you can't miss it. It just stares at ya.

(**THE STAGE MANAGER** *removes the automobile with the help of* **PA** *and* **ARTHUR**, *who go off waving their good-byes.*)

Well, come on upstairs, Ma, and take off your things. Caroline, there's a surprise for you in the backyard.

CAROLINE. Rabbits?

BEULAH. No.

CAROLINE. Chickens?

BEULAH. No. Go and see.

(CAROLINE runs offstage. BEULAH and MA gradually go upstairs.)

There are two new puppies. You be thinking over whether you can keep one in Newark.

MA. I guess we can.

(THE STAGE MANAGER pushes out a bed from the left. Its foot is toward the right.)

It's a nice house, Beulah. You just got a lovely home.

BEULAH. When I got back from the hospital, Horace had moved everything into it, and there wasn't anything for me to do.

MA. It's lovely.

(BEULAH sits on bed, testing the springs.)

BEULAH. I think you'll find this comfortable, Ma.

MA. *(taking off her hat)* Oh, I could sleep on a heapa shoes, Loolie! I don't have no trouble sleepin'.

(She sits down beside her.)

Now let me look at my girl. Well, well, when I last saw you, you didn't know me. You kep' saying: "When's Mama comin'? When's Mama comin'?" But the doctor sent me away.

BEULAH. *(puts her head on her mother's shoulder and weeps)* It was awful, Mama. It was awful. She didn't even live a few minutes, Mama. It was awful.

MA. *(looking far away)* God thought best, dear. God thought best. We don't understand why. We just go on, honey, doin' our business.

(then almost abruptly-passing the back of her hand across her cheek) Well, now, what are we giving the men to eat tonight?

BEULAH. There's a chicken in the oven.

MA. What time didya put it in?

BEULAH. *(restraining her)* Aw, Ma, don't go yet. *(taking her mother's hand and drawing her down beside her)* I like to sit here with you this way. You always get the fidgets when we try and pet ya, Mama.

MA. *(ruefully, laughing)* Yes, it's kinda foolish. I'm just an old Newark bag-a-bones.

(She glances at the backs of her hands.)

BEULAH. *(indignantly)* Why, Ma, you're good-lookin'! We always said you were good-lookin'. – And besides, you're the best ma we could ever have.

MA. *(uncomfortable)* Well, I hope you like me. There's nothin' like being liked by your family. *(rises)* – Now I'm going downstairs to look at the chicken. You stretch out here for a minute and shut your eyes. – Have you got everything laid in for breakfast before the shops close?

BEULAH. Oh, you know! Ham and eggs.

(They both laugh. **MA** *puts an imaginary blanket over* **BEULAH.***)*

MA. I declare I never could understand what men see in ham and eggs. I think they're horrible. – What time did you put the chicken in?

BEULAH. Five o'clock.

MA. Well, now, you shut your eyes for ten minutes.

*(***BEULAH*** stretches out and shuts her eyes.* **MA** *descends the stairs absentmindedly singing.)*

"There were ninety and nine that safely lay
In the shelter of the fold,
But one was out on the hills away,
Far off from the gates of gold…"

End of Play

Also by
Thornton Wilder...

The Alcestiad, or A Life in the Sun
The Beaux' Stratagem (with Ken Ludwig)
The Matchmaker
Our Town
The Skin of Our Teeth

<u>Thornton Wilder One Act Series: The Ages of Man</u>
Infancy
Childhood
Youth
Rivers Under the Earth

<u>Thornton Wilder One Act Series: The Seven Deadly Sins</u>
The Drunken Sisters
Bernice
The Wreck on the 5:25
A Ringing of Doorbells
In Shakespeare and the Bible
Someone From Assisi
Cement Hands

Please visit our website **samuelfrench.com** for complete
descriptions and licensing information.

OTHER TITLES AVAILABLE FROM SAMUEL FRENCH

THE ALCESTIAD, OR A LIFE IN THE SUN

Thornton Wilder

Drama / 18m, 4f, 1 boy, extras / Exterior

Wilder retells the legend of Alcestis, who gave her life for her husband Admetus, beloved of Apollo, and was brought back from hell by Hercules. Wilder's Alcestis is a seeker after understanding, to whom "there is only one misery, and that is ignorance." Her life as wife, mother, Queen is apparently tragic: idyllic happiness is destroyed by death.

OTHER TITLES AVAILABLE FROM SAMUEL FRENCH

THE SKIN OF OUR TEETH

Thornton Wilder

Comedy / 4 or 5m, 4 or 5f, plus many small parts w/doubling / Interior, Exterior

Winner of the 1943 Pulitzer Prize for Drama

This groundbreaking satiric fantasy follows the extraordinary Antrobus family down through the ages from the time of "The War," surviving flood, fire, pestilence, locusts, the ice age, the pox and the double feature, a dozen subsequent wars and as many depressions. Ultimately, they are the stuff of which heroes and buffoons are made. Their survival is a vividly theatrical testament of faith in humanity.

"Wonderfully wise...A tremendously exciting and profound stage fable."
– *Herald Tribune*